# OF SNOW AND ROSES

*A Magical Modern Fairy Tale*

## T.M. FRANKLIN

# Of Snow and Roses

## T.M. FRANKLIN

Cover images by:
stock.adobe.com
©Alex
Fantasybackgroundstore.com

Cover design by: T.M. Franklin

CALAVA
Press

Visit the Author's web site at www.TMFranklin.com

# CHAPTER ONE

The first thing she noticed wasn't a sight or a sound, but a smell: the pungent scent of disinfectant, used in an attempt to cover up something not nearly as pleasant. Not that disinfectant in and of itself was particularly pleasant in the first place. It stung her nose, coated her tongue, and made her sick to her stomach.

Then came a whispered murmur of voices.

"—think she's coming around. Be ready."

*Darkness.* And . . . and she couldn't move. Was she paralyzed?

Her heartbeat, a dull thud at first, picked up the pace as a trickle of panic ran down her spine. Where was she? Why couldn't she see anything?

Why couldn't she *move?*

"Can you hear me?" a man's voice asked.

She opened her mouth to respond but couldn't get any words to come out, so she nodded once instead. At least she could move her head.

"Good. Can you try and open your eyes?"

Ah, so that accounted for the darkness. It took tremendous effort, far more than it should, but she finally lifted her heavy lids, only to squeeze them tightly shut against the glare of light overhead.

"It's okay. Take your time," the man said, his voice gentle, soothing. "We're all here to help you. You're going to be all right."

After a few moments, her eyes fluttered open and slowly her surroundings came into focus. A sterile, white room with flickering fluorescent fixtures. A large window to her right, barred on the outside. She was lying on a bed and she tried to move again, eliciting a slight rattling sound. Her arms and legs were restrained by thick, padded cuffs attached to the bed. That was why she couldn't move.

A hospital? Why was she in the hospital? Why was she tied down?

Fear grabbed hold of her, stealing her breath, her chest tight as she gulped for oxygen and yanked against the restraints. Three people stood at the foot of the bed, watching her. Two men and a woman.

"Who are you?" Her voice was strange, raspy, as though unused for a long time, or perhaps strained by screams. The thought chilled her blood. "Where am I?"

"It's all right." The man in the center of the

little group took a step forward, hands held up. "We're here to help you. Do you know who I am?"

She had no idea, but he wore a white coat over his black button-down shirt and crisp black slacks. His hair was long and wavy, black with a streak of white, and brushed back from his face. His eyes were dark behind a pair of wire-rimmed glasses and he held a clipboard in one hand.

"A doctor?" she asked, muscles still straining as she tried to break free.

He smiled. "Yes, that's right. Do you know my name?"

"Why would I know your name? I've never seen you before," she managed to get out behind short, choppy breaths. Darkness edged in at the corners of her vision, the room growing blurry again, and her fingers tingling as she clenched and straightened them, twisting to try and escape.

"It's all right," the doctor said. "Please, try to calm down. You're hyperventilating and you're going to pass out. Inhale slowly, now, one . . . two . . ."

She tried to match his count, and gradually her heartbeat slowed though her hands remained in tight fists, her body tense and rigid.

"Where am I?" she finally asked. "What's happening?"

The doctor set his clipboard down on the narrow side table and sat on a metal chair next to

3

her bed. "What do you remember?"

She closed her eyes for a moment, searching for anything. "Nothing," she replied. "I don't remember—wait." Her eyes flew open. "Neve. My name is Neve."

The corners of the doctor's eyes twitched ever-so-slightly. "That's right. You're Neve. Anything else?"

She could feel the panic returning. "No. No—nothing. Why don't I remember anything?"

He reached out and touched her arm. "It's all right, Neve. Please try to stay calm and I'll explain everything, all right?" He glanced toward the other man still standing at the foot of the bed. He was tall and thin with stringy brown hair tied back with a bandanna. Like the woman, he wore blue surgical scrubs.

"I don't think we need the restraints, Calum," the doctor said.

The skinny man hesitated, casting Neve a nervous glance. "Are you sure, Doctor? She—"

"I'm sure," he replied quickly. "Neve's not going to cause any trouble. Are you, Neve? You understand that we're all here to help you."

Neve didn't understand anything, but she definitely wanted those restraints removed, so she nodded quickly. "I won't cause trouble. I promise."

"Good, that's good." The doctor patted her shoulder as Calum and the woman finally moved to unbuckle the cuffs. The relief at finally being able to move made Neve let out a little sigh as she rubbed at her wrists. The woman—short, stocky with red hair pulled into a tight bun at the base of her neck—adjusted the bed so Neve was sitting up.

"Now, first things first," the doctor said. "I'm Doctor Alberich and this is the Blackbriar Institute. This is Calum." He gestured toward the skinny man who'd moved to stand near the window, then to the woman, who smiled stiffly. "And this is Angelica. They're both nurses here."

Neve swallowed. "Can I please have some water?"

"Of course!" Doctor Alberich waved toward the woman—Angelica—who poured a glass from the pitcher on the side table and handed it to Neve.

She drank deeply, the water cool on her parched throat and tongue. When it was gone, she held on to the cup, turning it between her hands.

"Why am I here?" Neve asked. "Am I sick?"

Doctor Alberich frowned slightly. "Not physically, no," he replied. "But you've been here for years, Neve. And the amnesia is not unusual with your condition."

"Condition?" The word felt thick on her tongue. "What's wrong with me?"

The doctor hesitated, shooting a quick glance toward the nurses. "It's complicated, I'm afraid. You suffer from a multitude of issues that we've been treating since you were a young girl. This is not the first time you've lost your memories."

Neve's stomach fluttered with nerves, anxiety making her cold and clammy all over. She struggled to breathe deeply. Maintain control.

"Will I get them back?" she asked.

"Honestly, we don't know," Doctor Alberich replied with a sympathetic shake of his head. "It's possible, but—"

Neve swallowed. "But?" When he hesitated, she leaned forward and added quickly, "Please tell me everything. I can handle it."

He nodded and reached for the clipboard. "You never have before," he said. "You make new memories, but then another bout of amnesia occurs, and you lose those as well." He flipped through the pages of her chart. "You also suffer from hallucinations on occasion. Both auditory and visual. Delusions. Paranoia."

Blood rushed in Neve's ears as she slumped back against the pillows. "You're saying I'm crazy?"

"No," Doctor Alberich said firmly, his dark, fathomless eyes focused on her. "I'm saying you're ill. But we're all here to help you. You can trust us."

She looked around the little group, trying to read their expressions, searching their faces in the blackness of her memories. They all watched her patiently, waiting for her to absorb what she'd been told. To accept it.

Neve's initial instinct was to fight back. To shout that she wasn't crazy. Didn't have hallucinations and delusions and whatever else he said was wrong with her. She wanted to get up and walk out of that room, out of the hospital—what was it he called it? Blackbriar?—and keep walking until everything made sense. Run and run and run like she could somehow find her memories and snatch them back into her brain.

But where could she go? Who would help her?

Still, she couldn't simply accept what they said without at least asking for proof, right?

"How—" She cleared her throat nervously. "How do I know you're telling me the truth?"

Doctor Alberich let out a little laugh, and she noticed the nurses smiling as well. Neve stiffened, her hands tightening into fists.

"Sorry, Neve," the doctor said, noticing her reaction. "We're not laughing at you. I promise. It's just that you ask us that every time."

"Every time?" she repeated, stunned. "How many times has this happened?"

In response, he flipped back through her chart, then turned it toward her. Clipped to the top right corner was a picture of a little girl, perhaps five or six years old, wearing a flowy white dress. She was pale everywhere, as if all the color had been washed out of her—white-blonde hair in two braids hanging over her shoulders, creamy skin with a hint of freckles across her nose, and blue eyes so light they almost glowed. Doctor Alberich turned a few pages and she saw another photograph—the same girl but older, perhaps ten or eleven. Another few pages and there was the girl again, awkward and gangly with adolescence. Finally, on the most current page, a picture of the girl grown to womanhood, her pale eyes tired and worn, purple bruising the delicate skin beneath them. Her hair had darkened, but only slightly, gathered into a low ponytail drifting forward over her left shoulder, and she wore drab, colorless clothes, ill-fitting and unremarkable.

"That's . . . me?" Neve asked, reaching out a tentative hand to touch the picture.

"Yes," the doctor replied. "You've been here since you were a little girl. We've had this conversation six times so far."

Neve closed her eyes tightly, as if she could shut out the information. It was easier when she didn't know any of this, wasn't it? But the images of the girl burned behind her lids, and she knew there was no going back. After a long moment, she opened her eyes, a trickle of tears falling unnoticed down her cheeks.

"Can I get better?" she asked, feeling suddenly like that five-year-old girl, lost and alone.

Doctor Alberich patted her arm where it lay

limp on the bed covers. "We'll do all we can, Neve. I promise." He gave her a quick smile. "Don't worry. You're not alone."

She nodded, unable to speak with the clog of tears in her throat.

The doctor seemed to understand. "Now, I'm guessing you must be hungry. You missed lunch because of . . . well." He tipped his head with a sympathetic look.

Neve swallowed, putting on a brave face. These people had been trying to help her for years. The least she could do was try to be compliant.

"I am, actually," she replied.

He glanced at his watch. "Well, you're just in time for dinner," he said. "Calum will show you the way. We'll talk more later, all right?"

Neve nodded and got up from bed, slipping her feet into a pair of plain white sneakers she found tucked under the bedside table. She stood, giving Calum a tentative smile, but he turned without returning the gesture and led her from the room. She watched him walk, his thin frame angular and jerky, his own sneakers squeaking on the linoleum as they headed down a wide hallway with doors open on either side. Neve peeked into one as she passed. It looked exactly like hers—white walls, narrow bed, barred windows overlooking a grassy garden area, the light indicating early evening. Looked like summer, maybe? The grass was a little parched, the flower blooms a bit wilted.

She had no time to ponder the garden further as they turned a corner and entered a large common room with a scattering of a half-dozen round tables in the center. To the right, she could see a pass-through window to an institutional kitchen. To the left, french doors led out to the garden, and a battered upright piano crouched in the corner. A couple mismatched bookcases on the opposite wall housed some tattered volumes, and boxes of puzzles and games.

There were about twenty residents—patients, she reminded herself—sitting at the tables and eating, the sound of plastic utensils scraping against plastic trays a gentle murmur in the room. They all wore variations of what Neve assumed was the Blackbriar uniform: gray sweatpants, white T-shirts, gray hoodies and the same white slip-on shoes Neve wore. No color. No variation. No one spoke.

"Get your food over there." Calum motioned to the pass-through. "Sit anywhere but avoid Lily. The one in the middle with the weird hair." He smirked. "She bites," he said. Then he turned and left the room, hitching up his ill-fitting scrub pants.

Neve's stomach gave a nervous twist, and she avoided the curious glances of the rest of the patients, though she could feel their eyes on her as she walked toward the kitchen. An older woman with a white ponytail and piercing blue eyes popped her gum when Neve approached. She wore an apron with a smear of something across the stomach, and a name tag that read *Shelley* in fading black marker.

"Chicken or beef?" she asked, a large spoon poised over a pan of meat patties swimming in congealing gravy.

"Uh," Neve scanned the choices before her. "I'm not that hungry, actually. Could I have some of the potatoes and a little of the salad?"

The older woman grunted, although whether in affirmation or irritation, Neve wasn't sure. Shelley plopped a spoonful of mashed potatoes onto the largest section of the plastic tray and added a bit of iceberg lettuce mixed with shredded carrots in the corner. "Dressing's over there," she said, gesturing to a small table set up off to the right.

Neve added some ranch dressing and grabbed a roll and butter off the condiment table then, with a heavy breath, looked up to find a place to sit. The girl at the middle table with spiky pink hair, shaved close on the sides—Lily, the biter—smiled widely and waved at her. Neve knew she should find another place. She really had no desire to be bitten, after all. But the girl looked so friendly and eager, she couldn't ignore her. Hesitantly, she set her tray across from Lily and sat down, her hands in her lap and well out of biting range.

"Hi," she said.

The girl ripped off a piece of her roll and

popped it into her mouth, her teeth glinting as she chewed. "Hi, Neve," she said through a mouthful of food.

Neve blinked. "You know me?"

"Oh shoot!" Lily's nose wrinkled and she gave her head a little shake. "Doctor Alberich said you wouldn't remember. I forgot." She shrugged, like it was no big deal. "People around here forget stuff all the time."

Neve looked around the room at the others—a blonde woman in her mid-thirties crouched over her own meal, a short man with brown skin and a mustache talking with a slightly taller man who looked like he could be his brother. They were all ages—a gray-haired man was probably the oldest in the group, ranging down to a girl with short, black hair who didn't look more than twelve or thirteen. It was strange, wasn't it? To have children and adults in the same hospital?

What Lily said finally hit home. "Does everyone here have amnesia?" Neve asked.

Lily shrugged, and Neve finally noticed the rows of earrings curling up and around each of her ears, the colorful tattoos peeking out from the sleeves and neckline of her T-shirt.

"Sometimes," she replied before stuffing a huge chunk of meat into her mouth. Like that explained anything at all.

"You should eat," Lily said, eyeing Neve's

potatoes. "You won't get anything else until breakfast, and that's a long time."

Neve nodded and took a bite of the mash, subtly glancing around the room again. For the most part, everyone seemed to be ignoring her now, focused on their own food. She noticed a couple at the far table, talking quietly. It would have been impossible not to notice the woman, actually, a stunning beauty with russet skin, and thick, dark hair twisted in a braid that hung to her waist. She wore the same uniform as the rest of the patients but had thick leather bracelets around both wrists. Her face was heart-shaped, with sharp angled cheekbones and wide-set, dark eyes focused on the man to her right.

He sat curled over two trays, as if protecting them from anyone who might want to sneak a taste. He was huge, larger than Neve had first realized since he was hunched over, with thick arms and wide shoulders, meaty hands that looked almost comical trying to hold a plastic spork. His hair was brown and wavy, his face—what little she could see of it from this angle—covered with a heavy scruff, and he listened to whatever the woman said with an occasional nod.

Then, he stiffened, his hand curling into a fist and snapping the spork. The woman reached out and touched his hand, speaking to him in low tones, but he shook his head as if disagreeing with whatever she said. To Neve's surprise, the woman looked directly at her, then away just as quickly, leaning closer to talk to the man.

What was *that* about?

Unable to look away, Neve watched as the man seemed to tighten in front of her, muscles bunching, his jaw tense. He turned toward her, and for the first time, she saw his eyes—deep brown and focused intently on her. He seemed to vibrate in his seat, his gaze penetrating, pinning her in place. His lips parted, as if to speak, but his teeth were clenched tightly together in a painful grimace.

The woman said something sharply in his ear— something Neve couldn't hear—and the man looked away, back at the table. His body relaxed and Neve took in a shaky breath, unsure what had just happened, or if she'd imagined the strange, intensity of the man's gaze.

"You gonna eat that?" Lily asked, breaking her out of her daze.

"What?"

Lily pointed at Neve's roll. "You want your roll?"

"Oh, no." She pushed her entire tray across the table. "Help yourself."

"Awesome!" Lily gave a little dance and ripped into Neve's roll.

The couple across the room got up and walked toward the hall, not looking in her direction.

"Lily, who's that?" she asked in a low voice.

"Huh?"

Neve pointed with her chin toward the couple walking out.

Lily darted a glance their way, then piled some potatoes onto the remainder of the roll. "Oh, that's Torbin and Tala," she said.

"Do you know anything about them?"

Lily swallowed before responding. "Not really. Everyone around here kind of keeps to themselves, you know? Well, except me." She gave Neve an unsettling grin, all teeth. "I like people."

For a split second, Neve wasn't sure exactly how she meant that statement.

"I do know that Torbin doesn't talk," she said, starting on Neve's salad.

Neve leaned back in her chair, rubbing a finger along the edge of the cracked Formica tabletop. "The strong, silent type?"

"I guess," Lily said. "But I mean he doesn't talk. Like at all. I don't think he can." The lights flickered and Lily got to her feet.

"That's our cue," she said. "Gotta head back to our rooms for quiet time before lights out."

They lined up to bus their trays then walked out into the hallway. Neve still felt lost, untethered, and unsure what to do.

"I'm this way," Lily said, hitching a thumb over her shoulder. "You remember how to get back

15

to your room?"

Neve looked down the hallway. "Yeah, I think so."

Lily nodded. "Cool. See you at breakfast?"

"Okay."

The girl took off down the hallway at a near run and Neve decided that Calum the nurse had no idea what he was talking about. Lily seemed harmless. At least she'd been friendly toward Neve, and even if it was only because she wanted her dinner, she'd made no move to bite her.

Neve preferred to give her the benefit of the doubt.

She turned and retraced her steps toward her room and flicked on the lights, unsure how to fill the *quiet time* she had before her. She explored a little, opening the closet to find more sweatpants and T-shirts, underwear, bras, and socks in the drawers. That was it. No books, magazine, photographs . . . nothing to indicate she'd been living in this room for more than a decade. Neve was relieved the room had an adjoining bathroom, and that it was stocked with soap, shampoo, and towels, as well as a toothbrush.

She crossed the room to look out the barred windows at the grounds beyond, dully lit by lamp posts spaced evenly around the green on the edge of a forest. Neve tried to let her mind wander, hoping some lost memory would jump to the forefront if she weren't actively trying to push it forward.

But . . . nothing.

She had no idea how long she stood there, but eventually, there was a knock at the door and the red-haired nurse, Angelica, entered with a glass of water and a small paper cup.

"Time for your meds," she said, holding out the cup.

Neve held out her hand, more out of reflex than anything else, and the nurse tipped its contents into her palm. Neve examined the two white tablets, and a larger yellow one. "What is it?"

"The usual," Angelica replied, offering the water as she glanced at her watch impatiently. "Vitamins and Clozapine for your delu —" She pressed her lips together. "For your *condition*," she said. "Doctor's orders."

Neve took the glass and swallowed the pills, choking a little before she took another long drink. "Thanks," she said.

Angelica tipped her head in response. "Fifteen minutes until lights out," she said. "Better get ready for bed."

Neve brushed her teeth and washed her face. Then, unable to find pajamas or anything else that appeared to be sleepwear, she shucked her sweatpants and climbed into bed in her T-shirt. She lay staring at the ceiling long after the lights flicked off, searching the shadows cast by the outside lights. She was just drifting off when she sat up suddenly, uncertain what had alerted her. She had no idea what time it was—there was no clock in the room, no phone to check—but it was still fully dark outside, the lamp posts now out, the only light coming from the crescent moon overhead.

She slipped out of bed, the linoleum cold against her bare feet, and walked toward the windows, uncertain of what she was looking for. She pressed her hands to the glass, her breath steaming a circle between her palms.

All was still. The lawn lay empty save for the shadows of a few shrubs and scattered benches. The forest loomed dark and foreboding along the edge of the grass, an impenetrable wall in the darkness. Neve stood frozen, the hair standing up on the back of her neck with a frisson of awareness. Almost like someone was watching her.

What is it?

She narrowed her eyes, scanning the edge of the forest, looking for . . . what? She had no idea. Her gaze swept along the trees from left to right, then slowly back again, but there was nothing— wait.

Did something move?

Neve focused on the spot, willing the darkness to pull back, let her see whatever it was she was searching for.

Then, she saw it. A pair of golden eyes,

glowing in the night. And *there* . . . the looming shape of an animal, barely lit by the moonlight.

A bear.

It stepped forward out of the shadows, locking eyes with her, and Neve gasped, her hand flying up to her mouth.

But as suddenly as it appeared, it was gone. She searched the area frantically, but saw no sign of the animal, no movement. Nothing.

Had she imagined it?

She stood there for a long while, waiting for it to reappear, but it never did. Eventually, she slid back between her now-cold sheets, and finally fell asleep.

Somewhere in the darkness, he watched.

# CHAPTER TWO

Lily was waiting at the same table when Neve walked into the common room for breakfast. She waved wildly and pushed out a chair as soon as Neve grabbed her tray of limp french toast and sausage. With a nervous smile, she joined the girl, spreading a paper napkin on her lap.

"Morning," Lily chirped. "How'd you sleep?"

Neve opened the little packet of syrup and drizzled it over her toast. "Pretty good, I think. I don't remember waking up, anyway."

"Well, not that you would," Lily joked with a waggle of her eyebrows. "You know, the amnesia?"

Neve shook her head a little, smiling despite herself. "Yeah, I get it."

"Anyway, sleep's not usually a problem around here," Lily said as she chewed on the straw in her orange juice. "The meds, you know?"

Neve didn't know, but it didn't really surprise

her. She supposed most of the patients were medicated, if not all.

"I guess," she said, not knowing what else to say. She chewed on a piece of sausage as she surreptitiously glanced around the room. It looked pretty much the same as the night before, although there were fewer patients in the room. Other than Lily and herself, only the man and woman she'd noticed at dinner were there. What did Lily say their names were? Torbin and—she searched her thoughts, relieved when the memory came up easily.

Tala. Torbin and Tala.

"—don't you think?"

Neve realized she'd missed whatever Lily had been talking about. "I'm sorry, what?"

Lily rolled her eyes good naturedly. "I asked if you like group or solo better." At Neve's blank look, she added, "Therapy?"

"Oh!" Neve took a sip of her juice and considered. "I don't really know, actually. I don't remember."

Lily smacked her forehead. "Oh man, I'm so stupid," she said, smacking herself a few more times. "Stupid! Stupid! Stupid!"

"No, it's okay!" Neve reached out to pull her hand away, but stopped short and tucked her own hands under the table. "It's easy to forget." She gave the girl a little smile. "I should know."

Lily stared at her blankly for a moment, then burst out laughing. "Right." She giggled again. "Anyway, I should tell you then that after breakfast we have like an hour to ourselves for showers or exercise or whatever, then it's time for group." She leaned in, wrinkling her nose, the freckles standing out against her pale skin. "They won't make you talk too much at first, if you don't want to, but when you're in one-on-one with Doctor Alberich? He'll get all up in your business." She rolled a sausage up into a piece of toast and stuffed the whole thing in her mouth, not bothering to swallow before adding, "It's better to let him think he's helping."

"What do you mean?" Neve asked.

Lily swallowed down the mess of food with a gulp of orange juice. "Just go along with whatever he says," she replied. "It's way easier. A positive mental attitude is essential to recovery." She said the last in a mimicking type of voice, as if she'd heard it many times before.

"I don't—" Neve pushed away her tray, no longer hungry. "I really do want to get better," she said. "That's the goal, right?"

"Sure," Lily replied, wadding up her napkin and stuffing it into her plastic juice glass. "That's the goal."

Neve nodded, her gaze drawn when Torbin and Tala stood, bussed their trays, and walked toward the hallway. Torbin stiffened, as if feeling her eyes on him and turned to look at her. His own gaze darkened, a tick in his jaw pulsed and his hands curled into fists. He froze, staring at her, not moving toward her or away, just . . . looking. Neve felt pulled, somehow. Tied or locked in place. She couldn't look away and her breath caught, her own palms growing damp.

Tala grabbed his arm and hissed something into his ear. He nodded, finally breaking the weird connection between them and they walked quickly out of the room without looking back.

"What in the world?" Neve said on a shaky breath.

"Hmm?" Lily hadn't been paying attention, picking at a hangnail on her thumb.

"You didn't see that?" Neve asked. "That man. Torbin? He was staring at me." *And I was staring at him. Why?*

"Oh yeah?" Lily looked toward the empty doorway. "Well, he is kind of intense."

"I don't think he likes me."

"He doesn't really like anyone."

Neve swallowed thickly. "He looked like he *hates* me."

Lily tipped back in her chair precariously, fingertips on the table barely keeping her balance. "Listen, if there's one thing you'll learn while you're here, it's that people's moods are—what's the word?" She pursed her lips, thinking.

"*Mercurial.* That's it. We're all a little on edge, you know? I mean, we're *mental patients*. I wouldn't take it too personally. Tomorrow, everything could be completely different and you and Torbin could be best friends."

Neve doubted that, but Lily's words did ease her concern a bit.

"You gonna eat that?" Lily pointed to Neve's second piece of toast.

"Help yourself." She sipped her juice. "Hey, Lily, have you ever seen any animals around here?"

"Animals?" She peeled the crust off the toast, rolled it up and popped it into her mouth. "I think Angelica has a cat."

"No, I mean wild animals," Neve said, uncertain why she lowered her voice. "I could have sworn I saw a bear outside my window last night."

"A bear?" Lily's eyes widened. "I don't know. I haven't heard of that before, but we are on the edge of a forest, so I guess it's possible. You should mention it to Doctor Alberich. He might want to have animal control come out and take a look or something."

Neve nodded. It was probably nothing. And it couldn't have been as big as she'd imagined it, right?

And it *hadn't* looked right at her with glowing golden eyes. That was just paranoia. Sleep deprivation. An active imagination.

She refused to entertain the thought that she might actually be crazy.

"It's probably nothing," she said with a shrug as she got to her feet to bus her tray. "My eyes playing tricks on me maybe. Or—"

The room spun in a vicious spiral, walls, tables, and chairs blurring into a wash of color, and suddenly, Neve stood in a forest clearing. She gasped, stumbling slightly as she took in the towering trees, barren limbs reaching into the pale sky. The ground beneath her was soft, layered with needles and leaves, the scent of petrichor thick and sweet around her. Neve's hands trembled as she pressed them to her face. What had happened? Where was she? Had she lost more memories?

"Neve," a voice said from behind her.

She whirled around to see a woman standing there, dressed in a long, white gown, her feet bare against the forest floor. She was the same height as Neve, with pale skin and dark eyes, her hair a red so dark it was almost black. She held out a hand, palm up, and Neve saw a tattoo on her inner arm of a deep, red rose. It glinted in the shadows, nearly glowing, and the woman smiled at her.

There was something familiar about her, but Neve couldn't put her finger on exactly what it was.

"Who are you?" she asked.

"I'm Rose," the woman replied. "There's not much time. You're in danger, Neve. We're looking for you, but it's not easy."

"What? Who is looking for me?" Neve shook her head, confused. "What are you talking about?"

"Be careful," she said. "Don't trust him."

Neve's head swam with dizziness and she struggled to stay on her feet. "What? Trust who?"

The woman opened her mouth to speak, but the forest began to swim, black and white and red blurring in a spiral of color until the blackness bloomed, coating everything like a splash of thick paint running over the world, and Neve fell to the ground, overcome by it.

"Neve?"

She inhaled sharply, the scent of leaves and dirt replaced by disinfectant and greasy sausage.

"Neve, can you open your eyes?"

Her eyelids fluttered, and the room slowly came into focus. Neve realized she was lying on the common room floor, with Doctor Alberich kneeling next to her, a penlight in his hand.

"Don't move," he said when she tried to get up. "You may have hit your head."

He shone the light into her eyes, and she tried to follow his directions to look this way and that. Lily's pink head appeared next to his.

"Wow, you went down like a tree," she said.

*A tree? There was a tree, wasn't there?*

"Lily, that's quite enough," Doctor Alberich said, still focused on Neve's eyes. "You better go get ready for group."

Lily frowned but didn't argue and left the room.

"I don't think you have a concussion," he said. "Can you sit up?"

Slowly, she did, embarrassed to see that the kitchen staff, and Calum and Angelica were all gathered around, watching her. "I'm fine," she said. "I just—got a little dizzy?"

"Hmm," the doctor said, still eyeing her critically. "Are you sure that's all?"

Neve hesitated and the doctor frowned.

"Calum, can you help Neve up, please?"

"I'm fine," she said quickly. She got up and sat back down at the table. "Really." Neve's face burned and she was on the verge of tears. She may not have remembered much about her life, but she was certain at that moment that she hated to be the center of attention. "Please," she whispered.

The doctor took in a deep breath and studied her closely. "Could you all excuse us, please," he said to the people gathered around. As Lily had, they left without argument, and Doctor Alberich sat across the table from her. She studied the table, embarrassed and nervous, afraid to look him in the eye.

"Neve, it's imperative to your recovery that you are always honest with me," he said. "I cannot help you if you keep secrets."

Neve's shoulders hunched and she toyed with the frayed cuff of her sweatshirt. "It's nothing," she said finally. "I'm sure it's nothing."

"Why don't you let me be the judge of that," he said, leaning forward, his elbows on the table. "Tell me exactly what happened."

She bit her lip for a moment, then nodded. "I was sitting here, eating with Lily," she said. "And when I stood up, I got dizzy and everything kind of spun around, and then I was in this forest." She shot a glance at him, trying to judge his shock. Would he deem her insane? Wrap her in a straitjacket?

But Doctor Alberich simply steepled his fingers and tapped them against his lips. "Go on."

"I saw a woman." Neve crossed her legs and wrapped her arms around her torso, as if to protect herself. "She said her name was Rose."

At this, one eyebrow shot up, but the doctor gave no other reaction. "Did she say anything else?"

Neve frowned as she tried to remember the woman's exact words. "She said, 'We're looking for you.' And she said, 'Don't trust him.'"

"Trust who?"

"I don't know," she said through sudden tears clogging her throat. "I don't understand anything that's happening. I was there, then I was here. And it's. It's—" Neve scrubbed her hands over her face. "Am I crazy, Doctor? Hallucinating?"

Doctor Alberich gave her a stern look. "We

don't use the word *crazy*, Neve. So no, you're not." He leaned back, crossing his arms over his chest. "Can you describe this woman?"

"She—she was about the same height as me. Actually—" It suddenly hit her why the woman seemed familiar. "She looked like me," Neve breathed. "She had dark hair, dark eyes, but otherwise, she looked exactly like me. I can't believe I didn't realize—" Neve stared unseeingly out the window, picturing the woman in her mind, before turning back to him. "Why would she look like me, doctor?"

He removed his glasses, polishing them with a cloth he pulled from his trouser pocket. "I'm afraid this is all part of your condition, Neve," he said. "These delusions are not uncommon, and you have experienced them before."

"I have?"

The doctor replaced his glasses. "We may need to adjust your medication. But the important thing is for you to recognize what's happening."

Neve huffed out a wry laugh. "As if I have any idea what's happening."

Doctor Alberich gave her a sympathetic smile. "We can do many things to help you—with medication, with therapy—but you must make the choice to turn your back on these delusions. It's up to you to release them. Cut the ties."

Neve felt an odd mix of fear and hope. "How

do I do that?" she asked, almost desperate. She wanted to be better. She wanted her memory back.

She wanted to be *normal*.

"If it happens again," he said, "don't listen. Turn your back. Ignore it. Cover your ears and close your eyes if you must."

"Like a little kid?" she asked skeptically, pressing her palms to her ears. "La la la, I'm not listening to you?"

"I know it sounds ridiculous, but it works," he replied. "The first step is for you to take control of your delusions. That is how they will lose their power. Will yourself to be in control. To leave them behind. And we'll do our part to help.

Neve hoped that would be enough. "All right," she said.

At that moment, Angelica walked into the room with her little paper cup and glass of water.

"Ah, yes, this should help," Doctor Alberich said, taking the cup and handing it to Neve. "A slightly higher dosage should help you better combat the delusions."

Neve took the cup, and swallowed the pill with a gulp of water. It was strange that Angelica had turned up at that moment, wasn't it? How did she even know that Doctor Alberich wanted the medication? Had he said something Neve had missed?

She shook off the confusion as a wave of calm

trickled through her. It was probably standard procedure. They dealt with this all the time, right? And many times with Neve herself. She kept forgetting that they knew her better than she knew herself.

"Perhaps you should go to your room and rest," the doctor said, helping her to her feet. "Angelica will make sure you get there all right. You can join group tomorrow. I think you've been through enough for now."

The calm thickened, making her steps slow, her mouth clumsy. But that was all right. She nodded as Angelica took her elbow, leading her from the room. Rest sounded nice. She was rather tired, after all.

When she got back to her room, she slipped off her shoes and got on top of the covers, snuggling up to her pillow. Angelica left the room without saying a word, and Neve turned over to gaze out the window. A nap, then lunch. They'd help her. She'd be fine.

She'd be absolutely fine.

It was mid-afternoon before Neve woke from her nap, feeling groggy and a bit disoriented as she sat up in bed. It took a moment for her to realize that a number of patients were outside, some playing board games or reading ... others walking the perimeter of the yard. Neve hadn't even thought about venturing outdoors, but the sight of the clear sky and grass called to her and she quickly slipped on her shoes and went out into the hall, looking for the exit.

The french doors in the common room stood open and she walked outside, turning her face up to the sun with a smile. Inhaling the fresh air deeply, she felt almost normal, could almost forget she was in a hospital.

Almost.

A red gravel pathway wound alongside the building and around the large lawn, the lights she'd noticed the night before perched atop narrow posts at periodic intervals. She meandered along the path, watching a game of badminton in the center of the lawn. Again, she felt eyes on her, and glanced over her shoulder to find Torbin watching her from where he stood leaning against a tree at the edge of the forest. For once, Tala wasn't with him, and he stood motionless, tall and broad, his thick arms crossed over his chest.

*"Don't trust him."*

The warning from her vision—*delusion*—came to mind and she looked quickly away, ignoring the prickling along the back of her neck. She was sure if she looked back, he'd still be watching, but she didn't dare check.

Why did he seem to hate her so much?

Lily bounced up at that moment, her pink hair flopping from one side of her head to the other. She'd pulled up the legs of her sweats so her knobby knees showed, her pale legs as freckled as the rest of her.

"Feeling better?" she asked.

"Yeah," Neve replied. "Thanks."

"You missed lunch, so I grabbed you this." Lily pulled an apple from the pocket of her sweatshirt and tossed it to Neve as she fell into step beside her.

"Thanks," she said again, before taking a bite. "How was group?"

Lily shrugged. "Same as always. People talking about how depressed they are. Or how scared they are. Or how angry they are. Whatever."

"Which are you?" Neve asked, purposely not looking in Torbin's direction as they rounded the far end of the lawn and headed toward the forest.

"Me?" Lily laughed. "Oh, I'm none of the above. Just your average, run of the mill sociopath." She shot Neve a grin that was all teeth.

Neve snorted. "Calum said you bite."

"Only when people annoy me."

"Are you particularly annoyed right now?" The forest loomed, dark and thick before them, the crackle of the gravel louder than the laughter of the badminton game.

"Not particularly," Lily admitted. "Though I have to say it could change at any moment."

They were about to turn the corner and Neve would no longer be able to avoid looking in Torbin's direction. She held her breath and finally looked up . . . but he was no longer standing by the tree. She scanned the area quickly but didn't see him anywhere.

"Is this where you saw it?" Lily asked.

"Hmm? Saw what?"

"The bear," she replied, coming to a stop as she peered into the trees.

"Oh, that." Neve felt ridiculous about bringing up the bear. Most likely, it wasn't even real. Another weird delusion created by her off-balanced mind. "I think I probably imagined that."

"Did you mention it to Doctor Alberich?"

They continued down the path and Neve stared straight ahead as they finally did pass the spot where she saw—where she *thought* she'd seen—the bear. Maybe she should tell the doctor about it, but honestly, she didn't want more medication. It made her feel sleepy and loopy and—

No, she'd forget about the bear. It was another delusion, and what had the doctor said about them? Ignore them. Turn your back. Cover your eyes and ears if you have to.

That, Neve could do.

"Nah, it's no big deal," she finally told Lily. "I

think I was probably dreaming anyway."

Lily looked at her in surprise for a moment, then shrugged. "I'd probably stay out of the forest anyway. It's creepy. Who knows what's out there."

Neve finally gave into temptation and looked into the shadowy wood. "Do they even *let* us out there?"

Lily rolled her eyes. "It's not *prison*." Then, the strangest thing happened. Lily's brow creased; her lips turned down in confusion. "Is it?" she asked.

"What?"

Lily seemed to snap out of it and shook her head. "What?"

"You asked if—" At that moment a whistle blew, drawing their attention.

"Time to head in," Lily said, grabbing Neve's sleeve to pull her toward the building. "Craft Day. I love Craft Day!" She gave an excited little jump, and it was as if her moment of confusion had never happened.

*Weird.*

Well, it was a mental hospital, after all. And Lily was a patient. It would be weird if she *wasn't* a little weird once in a while, right?

"Oh, cool. Watercolors!" Lily squealed, and she dragged Neve to sit next to her, promising to share her brushes.

It was relatively pleasant, all things considered. Neve painted a still life of a drooping rose in a blue vase, then had dinner with Lily, who gave her the lowdown on all the other patients.

"—once ran naked through the building and Calum had to tackle him—"

"—and whatever you do, don't ask her about her mother—"

"—afraid of oranges, if you can believe that!"

She didn't mention Torbin or Tala, and Neve didn't ask. She hadn't seen them at craft time, or at dinner, and although she'd slept for hours after her little incident, she found she was exhausted by the time lights out rolled around. Neve took her meds and fell asleep, thankfully not tormented by delusions or dreams.

She was beginning to welcome the darkness.

Neve woke early, showered and dressed, and made her way to the common room for breakfast. Lily was sitting at her usual table, but looked different somehow. Her pink hair was tangled, she sat hunched over, and instead of inhaling her food, she simply stared at it. Neve got her own tray and sat down across from her. Torbin was staring— *again*—and although she didn't look directly at him, she could see his white-knuckled fist, his tense muscles, the tic in his jaw.

Then she noticed the bandage on the inside of Lily's elbow, another on the back of her hand.

"What happened?" she asked.

Lily didn't respond.

"Lily? Are you okay?"

Nothing.

Neve glanced around the room, looking for Calum or Angelica, but the only staff in the room at that moment, was the cook. What was wrong with Lily? She reached toward her.

"I wouldn't do that."

Neve jerked her hand back. She didn't recognize the warm, low voice, then realized it had been Tala who'd spoken.

"What's wrong with her?" Neve asked.

Tala simply shrugged. Torbin bared his teeth as if in pain, and she hissed something at him that Neve couldn't make out. He finally broke eye contact, his shoulders falling.

What was going on?

"Lily?" she whispered, ducking down to try and meet her eyes. "Lily, what's the matter?"

Instead of speaking, Lily began to rock slowly back and forth, then she lifted a hand and started to scratch at her wrist, lightly at first, then harder and harder, making white lines in the skin.

"Lily?" Neve thought she should find help. One of the nurses or Doctor Alberich. Lily began to scratch harder, and a small bead of blood rose in the wake of her ragged fingernail.

"Lily, don't. You'll hurt yourself." Neve grabbed her hand, intending to stop the scratching, but as soon as she touched Lily's skin, the girl let out a bloodcurdling scream and dove across the table at her.

"Lily. Stop!" Neve tried to hold her back, but Lily snapped her teeth at her, scratching and clawing toward her, continuing that unearthly scream. Her eyes were dark with madness, unfocused and crazed and she yanked Neve's hair, tilting her head back . . . baring her neck.

Then, she was gone. Neve blinked from the floor and realized that Torbin had crossed the room and pulled the girl off her. Lily continued to scream and thrash, wild-eyed, and Calum and Angelica finally ran into the room, the latter bearing a large syringe. She plunged it into Lily's arm, and the screaming finally subsided, although it seemed like the echo carried on far too long in Neve's ears. Lily crumpled to the floor and Torbin stepped back so Calum and Angelica could put her on a gurney and roll her out of the room.

It had all happened so fast. Neve sat on the floor, stunned, as Doctor Alberich spoke quietly with Calum in the hall before coming into the common room.

"Are you all right?" he asked her.

She realized she was still sitting on the floor and got up. Her scalp ached from the hair-pulling, but other than that, she was uninjured. "Yes," she replied. "What about Lily? What happened to her?"

The doctor frowned. "I'm afraid I'm not able to discuss another patient with you," he replied. "But rest assured that Lily will be getting the care she needs." At that, he turned on his heel and strode out of the room.

Neve watched him go, a sick feeling in her stomach. Poor Lily. She'd seemed fine the day before. They'd had fun. They'd talked.

What had happened?

She turned to look for Tala. The woman seemed to at least have some idea. And Torbin—Torbin had pulled her off Neve so quickly, as if he'd seen the attack coming.

But neither was in the room, and when Neve went to the french doors to see if they'd gone outside, she found them locked.

*It's not a prison. Is it?*

Lily's words sent a shiver down her spine, and Neve wasn't sure why. She didn't know what was real and what was delusion. Was she paranoid, or could there be a real threat at the Blackbriar Institute?

And if there was a threat, what was it?

*Don't trust him.*

Or maybe the question was: *who* was it?

# CHAPTER THREE

Lily wasn't at breakfast the next day. Neve sought out Doctor Alberich who only told her that Lily was in treatment isolation and could have no visitors. He wouldn't tell her anything more, or even how long she would be there. Lily would return when she was ready, he said, and Neve would have to be patient.

Something else Neve was learning about herself? She wasn't very patient.

She ate a bowl of cereal, went for a walk around the grounds, and nervously entered the common room when it was time for her first group therapy session. Seven patients sat in a circle with Doctor Alberich. Neve recognized a few: the young girl she'd noticed on her first day, Peter, an older man with a gray mustache who Lily told her had run naked through the building, and Torbin and Tala, who sat to Doctor Alberich's right.

"Come on in, Neve." The doctor waved her to

an empty chair next to the girl, who gave her a shy smile.

"Everyone, you remember Neve," he said, smiling at the group. "Unfortunately, she doesn't remember you, so let's take a moment for everyone to introduce themselves, shall we?"

The young girl was Alice, who turned out to be seventeen, not twelve, as Neve had thought. Next to her was an older woman named Nancy who crocheted while she talked. Then came Peter, followed by a thin woman with long, dark hair and trembling fingers named Melissa, and a short, squishy man named Adam.

Tala tossed her thick braid over her shoulder and crossed her legs. "I'm Tala," she said, not knowing Neve was already privy to that fact. "And this is Torbin."

The big man didn't look her way, but Neve saw his jaw clench.

And suddenly, it was all too much. Before she knew what she was doing, Neve bit out, "And does Torbin have some kind of problem with me?"

She swallowed. Had she really said that out loud?

Tala's eyes narrowed, any semblance of friendliness evaporating. "What makes you say that?"

Neve licked her lips, bravado slipping. "He seems kind of . . . angry."

"Well, he can't tell people when they do stupid things," Tala said through gritted teeth, "like touching a sociopath. So perhaps that gets a bit frustrating."

"All right, that's enough." Doctor Alberich intervened, holding up a hand. "Neve, I'm sure Torbin has no reason to be angry with you. Do you, Torbin?" He turned toward the large man, whose whole face seemed to tighten—Neve could swear she heard his teeth grinding—before he jerked his head slowly from side to side, then looked to the floor.

"Of course not," the doctor said, and was that a bit of a smirk on his face? But then it was gone, and Neve thought she must have imagined it. "Neve, I'm certain we all want you to feel welcome here, right group?"

Everyone nodded silently, except for the girl, Alice, who said, "Yes," in a quiet voice.

"Excellent." Doctor Alberich opened his notebook, pen poised over an open page. "Who would like to begin?"

Neve listened as Nancy talked about her anxiety, crochet hook flying over blue-green yarn. She snuck a glance at Torbin, who was still focused on the floor so she could study him a bit without him noticing. She was once again struck by how big he was—at least six-four, she guessed, with bulging muscle everywhere. His T-shirt clung to his chest, the hoodie unzipped over it, and for the first time she noticed the pendant he wore around his neck. She couldn't really make out the design from where she was, but it was metal—pewter perhaps, or worn silver, oval in shape and maybe two inches long. A hand wrapped around it and she realized he'd caught her staring. His eyes narrowed as he tucked the pendant inside his shirt and crossed his beefy arms over his chest.

Her face flooded with heat and she should have looked away—*wanted* to look away—but she didn't.

Couldn't.

*Don't trust him.* Had her delusion been her subconscious warning her away from this man, who obviously had an axe to grind when it came to Neve, despite what anyone else said? A reflex of self-protection since her memories had abandoned her?

"Neve, would you like to share?" Doctor Alberich asked, finally tearing her attention away from where Torbin glowered across the circle.

She really had no desire to share, but what was it that Lily had said? Give him what he wants?

Of course, Lily had then tried to tear her throat out, so perhaps any advice should be taken with a grain of salt.

Still, Neve *did* want to get better, and if this was part of her recovery, she'd do it. If there was any hope of regaining her memories, or simply preventing losing them all again, she would take it.

"Uh, I'm Neve," she said in a rough voice, searching for a friendly face in the group and settling on one, then another, while avoiding Torbin and Tala altogether. "I've been here for a while, although I don't remember it." She gave a little self-deprecating smile and a few of the patients smiled in return.

"I have amnesia, as well as a delusional disorder. At least that's what Doctor Alberich tells me. I'm, uh, sorry if I've done anything to any of you in the past. I honestly don't remember it." Heat rushed up her neck as her gaze dropped to the floor. Maybe that would be enough to appease Torbin. "I just want to get better and I hope we can be friends."

"That's very good, Neve," the doctor said, and Neve finally looked up to see him smiling at her. "We all want the same thing, so I think you're off to a great start." He checked his notes. "Who's next?"

Melissa raised a tentative hand and he nodded at her.

She was describing a nightmare she'd had when Neve felt a rush of dizziness and the world began to spin.

No. Not again. She clenched her eyes shut, and tried to breathe deeply, to ignore what was coming. But even though she couldn't see it, she could smell the pine and dirt . . . could hear the birdsong and the chirp of crickets.

"Neve." A woman's voice.

"No, I'm not listening to you." She pressed her hands over her ears. "You're not real. You're a delusion."

"Neve, stop that."

How could she hear her so clearly, even with her ears covered?

"Get out of my head!"

"Please, we don't have much time," the woman said. "I'm blocking him out, but I won't be able to for long. You need to listen to me. You're in danger."

Neve couldn't resist. Despite the warnings, she had to see. Had to know. She opened her eyes to find the same woman from before watching her with concern in her dark eyes.

"Why is this happening to me?" Neve asked, more to herself than anyone else.

The woman—Rose—smiled softly. "Be strong. You can do this."

"Do what?" she asked. "I don't even know why I'm talking to you. You're a delusion."

The woman scoffed. "I'm your *sister*."

"What?" Neve blinked in surprise. "No! No, you're a—I'm not going to talk to you. I'm not going to listen." She clenched her eyes shut, her fingers curling into fists. "Go away!"

"Neve, you have to listen!"

"No!" She could control this. She'd fight it off.

*Be normal.*

"I'm not listening," she said, murmuring quickly. "My name is Neve. I'm in the Blackbriar Institute. Today is—"

"Blackbriar?" the woman repeated, but her voice was fading away. "What's Blackbriar?"

"—*Tuesday.*" Neve said through gritted teeth. She could imagine if she'd open her eyes, she'd see the colors whirling, fading back to the familiar. She swayed back and forth and tried to ignore the dizziness.

"I'm in group therapy. We're having chicken sandwiches for lunch—" She was running out of things she knew. Things that were *true.*

So she started over.

"My name is Neve." Her voice grew stronger as the woman's grew quiet. "I'm in Blackbriar. There is no forest. My name is Neve."

"Neve?"

Her eyes flew open to find Doctor Alberich—as well as the whole therapy group—staring at her wide eyed. Neve blinked, taking in a shaky breath as she gripped the chair beneath her, worried she might collapse onto the floor again. She pressed her feet against the worn linoleum, focusing on the grounding feeling as the dizziness finally faded away.

"Neve, are you all right?" the doctor asked. "Do you need to lie down?" He waved toward Calum and Angelica who stood near the door and the duo started forward immediately.

"No." Neve held up a hand. "No, I'm fine. I promise. I just need a moment."

The two nurses paused, sending questioning looks toward the doctor, although they said nothing aloud.

"I really am fine," Neve said, forcing a smile. "I—I had a delusion." She glanced nervously around the group, worried they might judge her, but they only observed her with vague interest. She swallowed and looked to Dr. Alberich.

"I did what you said, though, and ignored it. I closed my eyes and . . . and I came back here."

The doctor pursed his lips and nodded slowly. "That's excellent, Neve. Good for you." He glanced around the circle. "Would you all please excuse us? That's enough for today."

The rest of the group left the room, and Doctor Alberich scrawled a note in his book. "I'm glad you were able to reject the delusion," he said, almost as if to himself. "But I'm concerned at the frequency. We may have to further modify your medication dosage."

Neve didn't like the sound of that.

"Is that really necessary?" she asked quickly.

The doctor stiffened, the air growing tense, and she realized that questioning him wasn't something that happened a lot.

*Give him what he wants.* Lily's words echoed in the silence.

"I, uh, I mean . . . the medication makes me kind of sleepy," Neve said. "Of course, I'll do whatever you think is best, Doctor." She forced a placid, trusting smile, even though her heart pounded with nerves and apprehension. "But I think I really have it under control. I can ignore the delusions and you said they'd go away eventually, right?"

She swallowed thickly, gaze dropping in what she hoped was a deferential manner. "I only want to get better."

He didn't speak for a long moment, and Neve gripped her chair, hoping he would agree. She truly believed she could do this on her own. Maybe it was ego, or perhaps pure stubbornness, but she didn't like being reliant on medication.

She also didn't like feeling like she was losing her mind, though, so if she had to swallow that stubbornness, she would.

"Of course you do," Doctor Alberich said finally. He stood and removed his glasses, tucking them into his shirt pocket and she finally looked up at him. Strange. Neve had thought him handsome when she'd first seen him, but now that she looked a little closer, she noticed his chin was a bit too sharp, his nose almost hawkish. Dark eyes probing . . . unsettling.

*Don't trust him.* The words were meant for Torbin, right? Whether a dream, vision, or delusion it seemed someone was trying to tell her something, even if it was her own subconscious. The truth was, Neve knew absolutely nothing about the world she'd woken up in. And perhaps she needed to be less trusting of *everyone* she came in contact with until she learned enough to know who actually had her best interests at heart.

Including Doctor Alberich.

She needed to protect herself. If she was—or was not—being paranoid would reveal itself in time.

"Perhaps we can wait and see about the medication," the doctor said, bringing her out of her thoughts. "We can reevaluate in a few days."

Neve smiled again, smooth and placating. "Thank you, Doctor. For everything." She stood, brushing invisible dust off her sweatpants. "I think I'll go and rest a bit before lunch?"

"Very well," he replied as he turned to walk out with her. "You'll let me know if you have any more episodes?"

"Of course, Doctor. And I promise to do what you said. Ignore anything I see that I know isn't real."

If she could figure out exactly what that was, she thought wryly.

They parted at her room and she watched him move away down the hall before calling out, "Doctor?"

He turned, eyebrows arched in question.

"Is there a chance . . . could I see Lily?" she asked, fingers twisting in the hem of her T-shirt.

The doctor frowned. "I'm sorry. That's not possible at the moment."

"I just . . . she's my only friend, and I want her to know that I care?"

He took a step toward her, head tilted. "She's not your only friend, Neve. We all care about you and want you to get better."

Her shoulder slumped at the quiet reprimand. "I know."

"And Lily will be back among you soon," he said gently. "Within a few days."

Deflated, Neve nodded. "Will you tell her I asked about her? That I hope she's doing better soon?"

"I will," he said briskly. "Now, go get some rest, and let me know if you have any more delusions, all right?"

"Yes. Of course."

With a satisfied nod, he turned to head down the hall, and Neve let out a heavy sigh. She hoped Lily was all right, but she had a strange, gnawing feeling in her gut that she wasn't. Neve couldn't explain it, but that was one item on a long list of things she couldn't explain right then.

She was about to go into her room and *rest*, although rest was the last thing on her mind, when a flash of movement down the hall caught her attention. Curious, she stepped quickly and quietly toward the corner where she'd seen someone disappear. She all but held her breath, willing whoever it was not to hear her approach. Neve hugged the wall, fingers tracing along the bumpy texture as she approached the corner, pausing before ducking her head quickly around it.

She didn't know what she'd expected. An empty hallway, mocking her paranoia, most likely. But instead, she came face-to-face, or rather face-to-chest, with the massive form of Torbin, who stumbled back in surprise from where he'd apparently been lurking.

"What are you doing?" she demanded. "Are you *following* me?"

His jaw tightened, but he gave a firm negative shake of his head.

"Then why are you hiding here, peeking at my door?" she asked, half-guessing but evidently correct if the flush on Torbin's face was any indication.

"Are you some kind of weirdo?" Neve pressed. "A stalker? Because I know self-defense, you know.

I don't care how big you are, I can take you down."

Neve had no idea if she knew self-defense or not, but assumed a fighting posture, hoping it would be enough to convince him.

He stared at her in surprise for a moment, then she heard a low, grunting sound burst from his lips. It took a beat for her to realize that he was laughing.

Torbin was *laughing* at her.

"What's so funny?" She lifted her chin, and her fists. "That's not—stop laughing!"

He held up his hands in a defensive gesture, although he still had a bit of a quirk to his lips. He had a scar, she noticed, that creased the right side of his upper lip, the scruff almost hiding it, but not when you got up close. His dark eyes studied her closely, his jaw still tight . . . in fact, all his muscles seemed tight. It was as if Torbin was always poised to spring away at any moment.

"Why are you here?" she asked finally. "Why are you angry with me? Why are you *watching* me?" Neve threw up her hands. "Why can't I remember? Why can't I—" To her utter mortification, tears sprung to her eyes and she inhaled sharply, trying to keep them at bay.

"Leave me alone," she said through gritted teeth. "If you can't stand me, stay away from me!" She intended to go back to her room but was stopped by a meaty hand on her elbow. She whirled back around and Torbin held up his hands again.

"What do you *want*?" she pleaded.

He pointed to the ceiling behind her and she spotted a camera in the corner. He pointed to another one in the opposite corner, and the pieces connected.

"They're watching?" she asked, and he nodded, then pointed toward the floor and shook his head.

"But this is a blind spot?" Neve guessed.

Another nod.

"Why are you hiding in a blind spot?"

His jaw tensed in frustration—she recognized it now for what it was—and he shook his head.

"Okay, then. Yes or no questions," she murmured. "Are you angry with me?"

He shook his head. *No.*

"You don't hate me."

*No.*

"But you have been watching me."

Hesitation, then a nod.

"And they—Doctor Alberich—is watching, too."

*Yes.*

"Not that unusual. It is a mental hospital, I'm sure—"

A grunt, and a vicious shake of his head. *No.*

"No?" she repeated, confused. "I don't understand."

But before she could ask another question,

Neve heard voices and footsteps coming toward them. Torbin stiffened and stepped away.

"Wait!" she called out in a quiet hiss. "Do you know what's going on around here? Where's Lily? Is she all right?"

Torbin shook his head, pointed to his eyes, then up at the camera, then at her.

A warning. *They're watching you. Be careful.*

Then he slipped away down the hallway and was gone.

Neve wasn't sure what to make of it. On the one hand, she was in a mental hospital, so Torbin was probably not a particularly reliable source. Still, there was something deep inside her that told her there was something to all of this. Something she was missing.

Something that was *wrong.*

It was so incredibly frustrating not knowing if she could trust her own instincts. To be aware that this could all be part of a paranoid delusion.

At the same time, she'd have been stupid not to at least question what she'd been told. Gullible. And with or without her memories, Neve believed she was anything but gullible.

So that left only one solution. To ask questions. Look for answers. Not raise suspicions and make up her own mind.

*Don't trust him.*

Oh yeah. That was a given. For the time being,

Neve wasn't going to trust anyone.

Neve wasn't certain what awakened her later that night. A strange squeaking—no, a *scratching*—at the window.

The curtains were closed against the lamplight, the room completely dark, so she switched on her bedside light and listened closely.

*There.*

It was quiet, but discernible now, and definitely someone scratching at the window. The scrape sent a shiver down Neve's spine and she swallowed nervously, blinking against the lingering wooziness from her meds. She slipped out of bed and padded tentatively toward the window, all the while wondering if she should jump back into bed and pull the covers over her head.

*Scrape.* What w*as* that?

The wind, she decided. It was the wind moving a branch or something. That's all.

Although there were no trees near her window. No bushes. Nothing that could account for—

"Oh, for heaven's sake, get a hold of yourself," she muttered as she reached out and yanked the curtains open.

A shriek burst from her throat when she saw an

enormous bear, right in front of her. It stood on its hind legs, towering over her by at least three feet. It had slipped a single claw between the bars where it scraped at the window, but when she screamed, it dropped to all fours and moved back from the window. Neve stood frozen, a hand clutched to her chest, as the bear did the strangest thing.

It looked right at her, then seemed to look over its shoulder before coming closer again and raising back up on its hind legs. Neve fought the urge to run, mesmerized by the bear's odd behavior. It reached out toward the window again—toward *her*—and tapped it's long, razor-sharp claw against the glass three times.

Then, it looked over its shoulder again, dropped to all-fours, and ran across the lawn and into the forest.

"What the—" Neve let out a shaky breath, running a trembling hand through her tangled hair. "What—"

Her door burst open, and the night orderly—Neve had yet to get his name—raced in, scanning the room until he focused bleary, dark eyes on her. Neve wondered if he'd been sleeping, too.

"What happened?" he asked, his voice raspy. "I heard a scream. Should I call Doctor Alberich?"

Neve wasn't sure what led her to say, "No. It's

okay. I'm fine," but she forced a self-deprecating smile and snapped the curtains closed. "I had a nightmare."

"A nightmare?" the orderly's brow creased as he looked from her over to the window and back again.

"Yeah, sorry to bother you." She decided to push through with the lie and not give him a chance to question it, slipping into bed. "I'm going to go back to sleep. I'm sure it won't happen again." She couldn't keep from glancing nervously toward the window.

"Oh, okay. If you're sure," he replied.

She simply smiled and turned off the light. The orderly yawned and left the room, and Neve found herself trembling again.

What in the world had just happened?

The next morning, she was almost convinced it had all been a dream. In fact, she'd pretty much decided that she'd imagined the whole encounter.

But when the french doors stood open after breakfast, she couldn't keep herself from walking outside, and heading toward her window. Nervously glancing over her shoulder to ensure no one was watching, she left the path and stepped closer to the bars, unsure what she was looking for until she saw it.

With a gasp, Neve reached up to pluck a piece of fur caught at the cross point between two metal bars—exactly where the bear had been scratching at the window the night before. Stunned, she stared at the tangle of black hairs in her palm, unable to deny the proof before her.

It had been real. A bear had been at her window the night before. Had looked right at her. Had seemed almost to try and *communicate* with her.

She felt ridiculous even thinking it, but how could she deny it now?

"You're not allowed off the path," Angelica's shrill voice drew her attention, and Neve quickly tucked the fur into her pocket before turning with a smile.

"Sorry, what?"

"The flower beds are off limits," Angelica said, popping her gum. "Residents must stay on the path or the lawn."

"Oh, yeah, sure." Neve quickly returned to the path. "Sorry."

Angelica shrugged, apparently not worried about pursuing the subject any further, and approached a group playing badminton. Neve spotted Torbin on the far side of the lawn, watching her carefully. She started toward him, but he subtly shook his head, warning her off.

Frustrated, she let out a heavy breath. If there was anyone who was more paranoid than Neve, it was Torbin. Still, she would find a way to talk to him at some point. She had a feeling he had at least some of the answers she sought.

For now, she clutched at the little piece of fur in her pocket and reveled in the fact that—at least in this one particular case—it seemed she wasn't crazy.

# CHAPTER FOUR

The next few days left Neve with a lot of time to think. The tedium of day-to-day life at Blackbriar was almost mind-numbing: Breakfast, Group, Lunch, Free Time, One-on-One with Doctor Alberich, Dinner, Bed.

Lather, rinse, repeat.

The mystery of the bear remained just that. She hadn't spotted it since that peculiar night when it had tapped at her window. But no matter how many times she tried to make sense of it, to convince herself that she was making more of it than it was . . . the more convinced she became that the encounter was more—not less—than met the eye.

Exactly what, however, remained out of her grasp.

She didn't tell anyone, not even Doctor Alberich, about the incident. She wasn't sure exactly why, however. He was her doctor, someone committed to helping her heal, but she couldn't shake off the feeling that there were some things better kept to herself, at least for now.

The bear was one. Torbin was the other.

He continued to watch her from afar but avoided coming close to her at all, let alone give her the opportunity to ask any of the millions of questions she had about Blackbriar and its staff and residents.

About herself.

Because Neve had a feeling that Torbin knew more about all of it than she could even imagine . . . but was leery to reveal any of it.

Not that he could. At least not out loud.

It was Saturday morning — four days after the bear incident — that something out of her new ordinary finally happened. She came into breakfast and noticed Torbin right away, sitting at his usual table on the far side of the room. His ever-present companion, Tala, however, sat near the door, alone at another table. She ate oatmeal like an automaton, scooping up and swallowing in a slow, even rhythm, her eyes staring off into the distance.

Neve stopped in surprise, her gaze darting from Torbin to Tala and back again in confusion. When she caught Torbin's eye, she raised her eyebrows in question, but only got the usual sharp shake of a head in response.

It was starting to get really annoying. She'd

given Torbin his space, but her patience was definitely wearing thin.

"Enough of this," she muttered, crossing the room in quick strides until she stood by his table.

"What's wrong with Tala?" she asked. "Did something happen?"

Instead of nodding or shaking his head, Torbin got quickly to his feet, picked up his tray and walked away.

"Hey! I'm talking to you." Neve trailed after him, barely resisting the urge to reach out and grab his arm.

She wasn't quite brave enough for that yet. The guy was *really* big.

He ignored her, set his tray on the counter, and walked out of the room. When she went to follow him into the hall, he whirled on her, eyes blazing.

"Oh, so I do exist," she said with a scowl. "I was beginning to wonder."

His jaw tightened, and she could tell he was grinding his teeth.

She glanced over her shoulder and lowered her voice. "I need to know what's happening around here," she said. "I have a feeling you know."

Torbin tensed even more, if that were possible, but eventually gave a quick, short nod, then a pointed glance to a camera mounted a few feet away.

"I get it," Neve said quietly, inching closer to

him. "But you can't keep avoiding me. If you want to stay under the radar, that's fine. But I need to talk to you."

He stared down at her for a long moment, then let out a hissed, irritated breath through his teeth. He gave her one more nod, then turned on his heel and stalked away.

Neve chose to take that as a good sign, but she decided she wasn't going to sit idle while she waited for Torbin to find a time for them to talk. Instead, she went back into the common room, got a bowl of cereal and a banana for breakfast, and set her tray next to Tala's, not even asking before sitting down. Tala turned to her in surprise, a spoonful of oatmeal hovering halfway between her bowl and mouth. Neve was once again struck by the woman's beauty, her shiny, black hair, high cheekbones, and smooth, tawny skin. Neve felt so pale and plain next to her, a piece of crumpled calico next to rich and vibrant silk. Still, she was on a mission.

"I don't think we've officially met," Neve said with a smile. "Well, outside of group, anyway. I know you're Tala. You're a friend of Torbin's, right?"

The woman didn't respond for a moment, her deep, brown eyes still slightly unfocused until she blinked, shaking her head as if coming out of a deep sleep.

"Who?" she asked.

Neve didn't know what she'd expected. Perhaps that the two friends had an argument of some kind. But Tala seemed genuinely confused by the question. Then it hit her. Perhaps Tala had a similar condition to Neve herself. Her smile fell.

"I'm so sorry," she said. "You don't remember? You have amnesia, too?"

The woman dropped her spoon into the bowl with a clatter. "I don't know what you're talking about," she said. "My memory is fine, not that it's any of your business."

Neve flushed. "Sorry." Tala was right, after all, but curiosity pushed her to ask, "But are you *sure*?"

Tala snorted and stirred her oatmeal before scooping up another bite. "I think I'd know if I lost my memory," she snapped. "I know who I am, where I am . . . why I'm here. Not that I plan to share any of that with a complete stranger."

"But what about Torbin?" Neve asked. "He's not a stranger. You two have always been together, at least as long as I can remember. But now —"

"Look." Tala stood abruptly and picked up her tray. "I don't know who you are, or who this *Torbin* is, but I don't have time for twenty questions, okay? I don't have any friends in here. I don't *need* any friends," she added pointedly. "So, no offense, but leave me alone, okay?"

"But —"

Tala heaved a sigh. "I'm sure you're dealing with your own stuff," she said. "Maybe you should ask Doctor Alberich about it? He can probably help."

She didn't wait for Neve's weak *okay*, before she turned and stalked away.

Weird.

In fact, the weirdness at Blackbriar kept stacking up: Torbin's secrecy, Lily's disappearance, and now Tala forgetting Torbin, despite the fact she seemed to remember everything else.

And on top of that, the whole scratching bear extravaganza. Plus, the delusions that Neve was starting to wonder were really delusions. She didn't have an alternative theory—not yet—but maybe there were more to them than she thought.

She sighed and peeled her banana, taking a large bite.

More questions. She hoped Torbin would at least be able to address some of them if she could ever pin him down.

Group that morning was the same as usual. Nancy crocheted. Melissa cried. Adam discussed his anger issues. Torbin and Tala sat on opposite sides of the room. He seemed even more tense than usual, and shot a few frustrated looks in Tala's direction, but she didn't acknowledge him once. After a quick lunch, Neve walked around the lawn a few times, grateful for at least a little fresh air. The seventeen-year-old, Alice, tried to lure her into a game of volleyball, but Neve wasn't up for it. Torbin loomed near the edge of the forest looking intimidating and tense.

But then, that was kind of his usual setting.

She felt his eyes on her as she ambled along the path, irritated at his constant attention. She couldn't make heads or tails of it, actually, and cast him a few annoyed glances of her own, hoping to deter him.

It didn't work. In fact, the next time she met his gaze, he lifted his chin ever-so-slightly, then jerked his head to the right, turning abruptly to walk into the shadow of the trees. Neve blinked in surprise, then quickly looked around to see if anyone had noticed Torbin's disappearance. Only Angelica and one of the day orderlies were on duty outside, and they were over by the french doors having some deep conversation of their own and didn't seem to be paying attention. Neve's heartbeat quickened, nerves taking flight in her stomach, but she forced herself to keep a slow pace, casually circling the lawn to the spot where Torbin had vanished. With one more quick glance behind her, she stepped into the shadows.

She hadn't noticed it, but there was a narrow path between the trees that she followed, her heart in her throat. Was she being impetuous? Definitely. Stupid? Possibly. She was going into the dark forest with a huge man who also happened to be a mental patient.

Neve was simply asking to be murdered, wasn't she? Talk about curiosity killing the cat.

Only a bare trickle of light made it through the canopy overhead, the shadows growing thicker the farther she went. Neve knew she should probably turn around, but there was no way she was going to, so she simply quickened her pace, following the winding trail. How far would it lead? Would there be a wall or fence? Barbed wire and electricity?

Neve barely held back a shriek when a hand reached out from the darkness and grabbed her arm.

"For heaven's sake!" she hissed when Torbin stepped into the weak light from above. "Are you trying to give me a heart attack?"

She caught a glint of teeth as Torbin grinned at her.

"It's not funny," she muttered.

His grin fell and he tapped the back of his wrist with two fingers.

*Not much time.*

"Okay, so I have questions—" she began, but he slashed his hand across the air, cutting her off, and tapped at his wrist again, more insistently.

Neve rolled her eyes. "Okay, *fine.*" She threw up her hands. "What do *you* want to talk about?"

He wrapped one hand around the opposite wrist, then switched to the other.

Like a pair of bracelets.

"Tala?" she guessed.

He nodded. *Yes.*

"Do you know what's wrong with her?"

*Yes.*

"What?"

Torbin went tense all over and bared gritted teeth. With a groan from deep in his chest, his shoulders fell and he shook his head.

"Okay then." Neve sighed. "Do you think she's in trouble?"

His eyes went bleak and empty. *I don't know.*

"Can't you talk to her?" Neve asked, then flushed. "I mean, not *talk*, but—"

Torbin shook his head. Firmly.

"Yeah, she wasn't really interested in talking to me either."

Torbin tilted his head, as if listening, then tapped his wrist again.

"I know. We'd better get back." Neve started toward the path, but he reached out and grabbed her elbow, then mimed putting something in his mouth.

Neve stared blankly at him for a moment, and he repeated the motion.

"Okay, I don't remember, but I'm pretty sure I'm bad at charades," she muttered, sighing when he kept doing the same thing. "Food?" she guessed.

He shook his head. *No.*

"Okay, not food," she said. "Umm, candy?

Water? Uh, what else do you put in your mouth?"

He pointed at her and nodded. *Yes.*

"Something you put in your mouth," she said.

He nodded.

"But not food."

He shook his head. *No.*

"Not something you eat?"

*No.*

"Something you drink?"

*No.*

"Well, what in the world do you put in your mouth that you don't eat or drink?" She huffed in frustration. "Gum?"

He sighed heavily. *No.*

"Medicine?"

He pointed and nodded, a wide smile on his face.

"Medicine," she repeated, matching his smile. "Okay, what about it?"

He shook his head violently.

"No?" She frowned at him. "No medicine?"

He nodded.

"You—" Neve's eyes narrowed. "Are you telling me not to take my medication?"

He nodded again. Slowly and emphatically.

"But why?"

His head snapped up as if he heard something and he tapped his wrist again before moving past her down the path.

*Out of time.*

"No, wait!" she called out, and he whirled around, pressing a finger to his lips.

"Sorry," she whispered. "But I need to ask—"

He tapped his wrist twice—hard—then pointed back toward the Institute. They'd been gone too long. Someone was going to notice they were missing.

"Fine, okay." Neve fell into step behind him as they hurried back down the path. "But I am going to have my questions answered eventually. You might as well accept the fact that I'm not giving up."

He grunted—maybe more like a laugh—and once again, Neve wondered how much Torbin knew.

How well he knew *her.*

And the instant that thought crossed her mind, she had a flash of something akin to realization. Acceptance. Something falling into place.

Before she could dwell too much on it, though, they neared the edge of the forest, and Torbin held up a hand to stop her at the sound of voices.

"—scratched up my arm, but good. Look at it."

Calum was talking to someone, and they were nearing Torbin and Neve. They both moved back silently to be better hidden.

"She is a wild one," Angelica replied. "But I don't think she'll be causing any more problems."

Neve wanted to know who they were talking

about, but she held her breath, more worried about getting caught. Neve caught sight of them through the brush and took another step back.

*Crack!* She froze as a small branch broke beneath her foot, afraid to move another muscle.

"Did you hear that?" Calum asked.

"Hear what?"

Neve could see them both now, about four feet to the left of the path. Angelica was frantically trying to light a cigarette, red head bowed and hand curled around the flame. Calum was looking to the forest—right in Neve's direction—his eyes narrowed as he peered into the darkness.

Could he see her?

Neve held her breath and closed her eyes. Torbin's fingers slowly circled her wrist, pressing gently.

*Don't move.* It couldn't have been any clearer if he'd said the words aloud. His touch reassured her somehow. Comforted her. At least she wasn't alone.

*Don't see us.* Neve clenched her eyes shut, wishing. *Please don't see us.*

"I could have sworn—" Calum muttered, but a shout from the volleyball game drew his attention, and the pair whirled and hurried over to break up an argument over whose turn it was to serve.

Neve released a shaky exhale and opened her eyes, peeking around Torbin's bulky form to see Angelica and Calum turned away from them.

Torbin pulled her forward, still gripping her wrist, then pushed her gently toward the path.

"This isn't over," she hissed as she hurried out onto the path bordering the lawn, then slowed to a more leisurely stroll. A few moments later, she heard Torbin do the same, heading away from her. When her heartbeat finally slowed and she dared to look back, he stood leaning against a tree again, arms crossed over his chest as he watched the volleyball game resume.

She knew she should ignore his advice, of course. The last thing she should do is stop taking the medication prescribed for her by her doctor—medication that was supposed to stop her delusion and help her regain her memory.

But—

But that falling-into-place feeling she'd had when she thought that perhaps Torbin might know her? She had the same feeling when she thought about stopping the meds. And although she knew between now and bedtime, she'd argue both sides viciously, leaning first one way, then the other. Deciding to follow Torbin's advice, then vehemently to ignore it.

In the end, she would do the only thing she could; hide those pills under her tongue and flush them down the toilet.

That night, she dreamed of Rose.

Neve found herself lying in the same clearing, below the same barren, towering trees, washed in the same milky, gray shadows. She could feel the dirt and rotting leaves beneath her fingers, the cool air on her skin. It was so vivid, so real . . . so different from any dream she'd ever had before that her guard was down and she didn't even think of trying to fight off the delusion. Instead, she got to her feet and inhaled the sweet, mossy air, reveling in the quiet sounds of the forest around her.

It was peaceful. For a moment, she could forget about Blackbriar, about her illness, about Torbin and Lily and Tala and everything that had been weighing so heavily on her mind.

She could *breathe.*

"Neve."

She whirled to find Rose standing behind her, in the same white gown, a tentative smile on her face. Now that Neve could study her more closely, Neve saw the resemblance to herself, like a negative image from a camera—the same pale skin dotted with freckles, upturned nose and slightly pointed chin. It was like looking into a mirror except for the dark red hair and fathomless, ebony eyes, and when Neve smiled, Rose did at the same time, accentuating the illusion.

"I should ignore you and try to wake up," Neve said. "But it's kind of nice here."

Rose's smile grew as she looked up at the trees. "It is, isn't it? Good job."

"Good job?" Neve huffed out a laugh. "What's that supposed to mean?"

Rose met her gaze once again. "Well, I reached out to you, but this—" She waved a hand around her in a slow circle. "This is all you. You created a place where you feel comfortable."

"But that—" Neve shook her head. "That doesn't make any sense. Created it how?"

Rose frowned. "Wait—You don't know?"

At that, a surge of frustration rose up so strong, so vicious, that Neve snapped, "No, I don't *know*! I don't know anything! I don't know who I am, or where I came from. I don't know you. I don't know this place—" She threw up a hand and started to pace angrily. "I don't know what's happening to me, or why I'm crazy—"

"You are *not* crazy," Rose said emphatically.

"Like I'm supposed to accept the word of a figment of my imagination!" Neve snorted.

"A figment—" Rose, for the first time, moved from her spot by the tree and approached Neve. "Wait a minute. I thought he had confused you somehow. He's good at that. But are you telling me you don't know me? You don't remember me at all?"

"Of course I don't remember you! I don't remember anything!"

Rose cursed under her breath, pressing a hand to her lips. "I can't believe this."

"*You* can't believe it?" Neve huffed out a humorless laugh. "I'm living it and I can't believe it."

"Neve, you have to listen to me." She cocked her head, as if hearing something in the distance. "I can't keep this up for long. The connection is already weakening."

At that, Neve noticed the edges of the forest growing blurry, smearing like paint again.

"What's happening?"

"Listen!" Rose replied sharply. "I am your *sister*. We're looking for you and we will find you. Be strong until then."

"We? Who—"

"There's no time to explain," she interrupted. "What can you tell me about where you are?"

"Where?" Neve swallowed, glancing up nervously as the blurry edges grew closer. "I'm in my room at Blackbriar."

"Anything else?" Rose asked quickly. "Do you know where Blackbriar is?"

Neve's head was beginning to ache, and she rubbed at her temples. "No. There's a forest surrounding it. That's all I know."

Rose crossed to Neve in two steps and reached out to grasp her hands. Surprisingly, Neve could feel her touch.

"You have to try and get out of there," Rose said. "But don't let him know. You can't let him know you're on to him. Whatever you do, don't trust him."

She felt a surge of guilt at that . . . of nervous doubt, even though the woman — the *dream*, for heaven's sake, she was feeling guilty talking to a *dream* — could have no idea that Neve had spoken to Torbin.

Still, even though this was most likely all in her head, Neve felt an unexplainable urge to reassure her. "I haven't even gotten near him," she said. "I'm pretty sure he hates me, so don't worry."

"Oh, he *definitely* hates you," she replied with a little laugh. "But he hasn't tried to talk to you? He hasn't . . . *done* anything to you?"

"No?" Neve tilted her head in confusion. "I don't think Torbin would —"

"Torbin?" Rose's dark eyes widened. "*Torbin* is there with you? Nobody's been able to find him, but we thought he was off searching for you!"

"I don't understand —" The forest began to swim, green and black and gray smearing like paint on a canvas, but Neve could still feel Rose's hands on her arms, squeezing them, shaking them slightly.

"You have to talk to Torbin," she said urgently. "He can help you but be care—"

"But you said not to trust—"

"Here, this may help," Rose said quickly, pushing up her sleeve so her rose tattoo came into view. She ran her fingers over it, then reached for Neve's left arm, tracing the same area on her skin. Too stunned to pull away, Neve watched as the iridescent outline of a snowflake appeared on her arm. It sparkled as if lit from within, and a trickle of heat creeped out from under it, up her arm and down to her fingertips.

"Be careful." Rose squeezed both her hands. "I love you."

And with that, the swirling closed in, swallowing Neve in darkness. She awoke with a gasp, back in her bed, the weak stream of early dawn sunlight peeking through the edge of the curtains.

Heart pounding, she pushed back the covers and shoved up her sleeve, gasping at the sight of a fading snowflake, shimmering against her skin. It flared as she touched it, growing a little brighter, sparks of pale blue, pink, and white snapping off her fingertips. With a gasp, she clenched her hand into a fist, clutching it to her stomach in reflex as she curled in on herself. Breath quickening into rapid pants, a counter melody to her rabbiting heartbeat, she closed her eyes and tried to keep from passing out.

She could do this.

*Just breathe. In and out.*

After a while, when Neve was no longer in danger of fainting, she opened her eyes. The room was cast in shadow by the dim light piercing the gap in the curtains, and she took a moment to ground herself in reality.

The bed. The table. Her sweatshirt draped over the chair on the opposite side of the room.

Then, ever-so-slowly, she straightened and extended her arm. The sleeve had dropped back down again, the frayed edge brushing her wrist, and she licked her lips, hesitating before she reached out and pushed it up to her elbow, revealing the pale skin underneath.

Nothing.

She jerked her arm closer to her eyes, frantically searching for any sign of the glowing lines, the twinkling colors, but they were gone. No glowing. No sparks. No snowflake.

"What in the world?" she muttered, running a palm over the bare skin. "Am I losing it?"

But no.

There was . . . *something* there. Nothing Neve could see, but she could swear that the skin on the inside of her arm felt warm.

Tingling.

The feeling slowly faded, but she sat staring at

the spot for a long time, until the room lightened, and the sounds of morning activity filtered in from the hall.

What was going on?

The more Neve tried to make sense of it, the more her thoughts kept going in circles. If she *was* delusional, then it was all in her head. On the other hand, she'd found proof that at least *some* of it was real. She had the bear fur, after all.

And if she *wasn't* delusional, why was she in a mental hospital in the first place? And why couldn't she remember anything?

With every passing moment, Neve became more convinced that it wasn't all in her head. What she couldn't figure out was how all the pieces fit together.

And when she finally dressed and made it to the common room for breakfast, yet another piece of the puzzle was sitting at the table in the center of the room, munching on a piece of toast slathered with strawberry jam.

Lily was back.

# CHAPTER FIVE

Neve's first instinct was to run over and talk to Lily, ask what had happened, and make sure she was okay. But she hesitated, remembering her last interaction with the girl. Lily had been almost animalistic, teeth bared and eyes wild, and Neve definitely didn't want a repeat of that incident.

After almost a week, though, she was incredibly relieved to see her.

Lily seemed a bit pale and tired, the usually spiky, pink hair on the top of her head hanging limp and lifeless . . . dark circles bruising the skin under her eyes. She munched on her toast, interspersing bites with gulps of milk, but didn't seem to pay attention to anyone or anything around her.

Neve got her tray, haphazardly grabbing a bowl of cereal and an apple, and approached the table warily. She was aware of Torbin watching her from across the room . . . of Tala completely ignoring her from her place near the door.

Neve cleared her throat. "Mind if I sit here?"

Lily jumped a little, as if she'd been lost in thought. "It's a free country," she replied with a shrug.

Neve swallowed, still unsure of her reception. "How are you feeling?"

Lily darted a calculating glance at her. "Who wants to know?"

So she didn't remember. Well, Neve could relate to that.

"I'm Neve," she said, twisting the stem off her apple. "You, uh, look better than the last time I saw you." It was a lie — she looked terrible — but at least she wasn't trying to rip Neve's head off.

"Uh, thanks? I guess?"

Neve smiled, her tense shoulders relaxing slightly. "I'm glad you're back," she said. "It wasn't the same around here without you."

Lily sat back, swiping a smear of jelly from the corner of her mouth with her thumb before licking it off. Her eyes narrowed on Neve for a moment, before she focused on the table top. "I wouldn't know."

There was something so . . . *passive*, about Lily now. Her carefree smile and dancing eyes were nowhere to be found, and she considered Neve with a nervous, almost frightened air, quick glances skirting away whenever their eyes met.

"Doctor Alberich said you were in treatment," Neve began.

"He talked to you about me?" Her voice trembled a bit, and she looked on the verge of tears. "Why would he talk to you about me?"

"He didn't," Neve said quickly. "Not really. I was just really worried, and—" She set the apple back on the tray, unsure of how to proceed. There were so many things she wanted to know, but it was pretty evident that Lily was in no condition to share them.

She decided to change tactics. "Do you have any idea what happened to you?"

Tears filled Lily's eyes. "I don't know."

"Where you were? What kind of treatment—"

"I said I don't know!" She stood and picked up her tray, fumbling it in her trembling hands. "Why are you asking me all these questions?"

"I'm only trying to figure out what happened." Neve got to her feet and moved around the table slowly. "Please, Lily, can you remember anything? It might be important."

"Can you leave me alone?" Lily said, her voice taking on a frantic tone. "I need to go to my room."

"Lily—"

"What's going on here?" Calum stalked across the room, moving between them. "You both need to calm down."

"I am calm," Neve replied through gritted teeth,

frustration making her impetuous. "But I want to talk to Lily."

"I don't want to talk to *her*," Lily told Calum. "Can you make her leave me alone?"

Neve's own throat choked with tears, everything she'd been thinking and feeling and *living* suddenly an unbearable weight on her shoulders. Lily was her friend. She only wanted to help.

"Where has she been?" she asked Calum. "She's been gone for so long, and now she's—" She waved a hand. "—different. What did you do to her?"

Lily was completely freaked out now, silent tears streaming down her face. "What's she talking about?"

"Nothing," Calum said soothingly. "It's all right."

"It's *not* all right," Neve snapped. "It's like Lily's had a personality transplant . . . and Tala!" She pointed to where the woman sat, oblivious to the happenings right in front of her. "Tala's been acting strange, too. Something weird is going on here."

"I don't like this," Lily said, whispering through her tears to no one in particular. "I want to go to my room."

"Lily, listen to me—" Neve tried to step around

Calum, but he matched the movement, blocking her.

"Let me *talk* to her," she exclaimed, exasperated.

"No!" Lily said.

"I think you need to go back to your room," Calum said, wrapping his thin fingers around Neve's elbow. "Come on, let's go."

She yanked her arm away. "Don't touch me."

"I said, let's go." Calum grabbed her by the wrist this time, his grip tight and demanding. "Unless you want me to get the restraints—"

The thought of being tied down again sent a rush of panic through Neve, and her heart fluttered in her chest. "No," she said. "Don't do that."

Lily was rocking slightly, curled in on herself, and suddenly, Torbin was there, wedging his way into the bizarre tableau.

"This is not your concern," Calum said through a sneer. "So unless you want me to call Doctor Alberich, I suggest you step back."

Torbin didn't move. Lily continued to rock, and Neve's breathing quickened, her skin heating as she tugged against Calum's grip.

"Angelica, get the Haldol," Calum called out, "and the restraints."

"No!" Neve shouted, a surge of tingling heat running through her as sparks erupted from her fingertips. Calum released her with a gasp and she quickly clutched her arm to her stomach, hiding it in the folds of her sweatshirt.

"What did you do?" Calum exclaimed. He'd been looking away when it happened, so he hadn't seen the sparks, but he definitely *felt* something. He started toward her, but Torbin loomed in his way, shaking his head ever-so-slightly.

"Move," Calum growled at him. "Or you will regret it."

"Torbin, no." Neve said quietly. "It's okay." She forced herself to breathe evenly, willing her heart to slow. She could feel it when the heat and tingling receded, and when she extended her hand to touch him, the sparks were gone.

Another point for the *Weird Stuff That Was Actually Real* column.

She didn't have time to dwell on it, however.

"I'm sorry," she told Lily. "I didn't mean to scare you." Then to Calum, "I got a little upset, but I promise, I'm all right now."

He studied her. "But what did you do to my arm?"

She shrugged. "Static electricity, I guess. Sorry?"

"Strongest static I've ever felt," he muttered, but he stepped back, waving her forward. "I think everyone needs to spend a little time in their rooms." He glared at Torbin. "I'm pretty sure Doctor Alberich will want to talk to you."

They filed out of the common room and went

their separate ways, Torbin sending Neve a significant look before he turned and walked away. She wasn't sure if it was a *We'll talk later* look or a *Wow, you really messed up this time* look—probably a combination of both—but Neve was pretty sure this wasn't the end of it.

She couldn't think about that at the moment, though. Because she'd just seen something incredible happen, and now she knew it was real.

Calum had felt it. She was pretty sure that Torbin had seen it.

She'd done *something*, although she still wasn't certain exactly what it was. But it felt familiar to her now, and Neve was pretty sure she could do it again. Not with Calum dogging her heels, however. The man trailed after her, apparently unworried that Lily and Torbin would follow directions, but unsure if Neve would.

Doctor Alberich was waiting at her door when they arrived. "Hello, Neve," he said. "I understand there was a bit of a commotion at breakfast."

Neve forced a smile. "It was nothing, really. I wanted to talk to Lily, but she wasn't up for it."

He frowned and exchanged a significant look with Calum. "No, no. I would think she wouldn't be," he said. "Would you please go inside? I'd like to speak with Calum for a moment."

Neve wanted to argue. She *really* did. But she knew better.

"Yes, Doctor," she said before entering the room. He closed the door firmly behind her and she pressed her ear against it. All she could make out was the low rumble of voices, however.

"Come on, speak up," she muttered to herself. "I want to hear you."

To her surprise, the voices grew louder—maybe they'd moved closer to the door—and she could clearly hear their conversation.

"—need to adjust her meds," Doctor Alberich said. "Tell Angelica to double the dose."

"What are you going to tell the girl?" Calum asked.

He let out a little laugh. "I don't have to tell her anything," he replied. "I'm her *doctor*. I have her best interests at heart."

At that, the two men walked away, and Neve let out a shaky breath. She crossed to her bed and climbed onto it to sit cross-legged, slipping off her sweatshirt. She rested her hands on her knees, palms up, and looked down at them, chewing her lip. They looked . . . normal. Pale skin and blue veins . . . bone and muscle and blood.

But they weren't normal. Nothing about this situation was normal. Neve was finally beginning to understand that.

She needed to be more careful. With Doctor Alberich and Calum watching her more closely—*doubling* her meds—it was going to be harder to pretend she'd taken them. Harder to get rid of them.

Harder to hide whatever was happening to her.

Neve was confined to her room for the rest of the day. She didn't know if the others had a similar punishment—*opportunity for insight and growth*, according to Doctor Alberich—because, as usual, nobody would tell her anything.

Her meals were brought to her, and she ate sitting on her bed, not really tasting the food. She watched the others outside during free time but didn't see Lily or Torbin among them. It gave her a lot of time to think, although whether that was a positive or a negative, Neve wasn't quite sure.

When night fell, Angelica brought her medication—double the pills, Neve noticed without mentioning it—and she made a good show of pretending to swallow them, wishing desperately the whole time that Angelica would buy it.

She did. The nurse watched her dispassionately, then left the room and Neve spat the pills in the toilet.

Although it left her clearer, the downside was a

difficulty in falling asleep. It was past midnight when Neve was lying in bed, staring at the shadows flickering on the ceiling, and she heard a scratch at the window.

She stiffened, and after a long moment, she heard it again.

Goosebumps broke out across Neve's skin as she slipped quietly from under the covers. The floor was cold against her bare feet, and she rubbed her arms, all but tiptoeing toward the window. The curtains swayed slightly in the faint current from the heating ducts, the gap between them widening and narrowing in a slow rhythm. She took a steadying breath and reached out to pull them open.

Neve knew what she'd see, of course, but it was still startling to come face to face with an enormous bear. She gasped, heart racing as she stumbled back a few steps. It took a moment for her to regain her composure.

The bear waited patiently . . . if bears were capable of such a thing, and watched as she approached.

"Back again, huh?" she murmured. "Boy, you're a big fellow."

It stood on its hind legs, towering over her, one claw shoved through the gap in the bars. It looked down at her, but didn't move, its eyes black and shadowed in the darkness.

"What do you want?"

The bear dropped down to all fours and tipped its head—now even with Neve's—to the side, as if in question.

She placed her hands flat on the glass and leaned closer, curiosity winning out over fear. The bear turned as if to leave, walked away a few steps, then looked back over his shoulder. After a few moments, he came closer again, then repeated the walk away and look back.

"Are you—" Neve couldn't believe she was talking to a bear. "Do you want me to follow you?"

When it simply stared at her, she laughed. "Okay, Neve, you're losing it," she mumbled. Even if it were some kind of circus bear that understood English commands—Hey, that could be a thing!—it couldn't possibly hear her through the glass. Her imagination was definitely running away with her.

"I wish I could," she said, suddenly overcome with a wave of longing. "I wish I could follow you right out of here and go somewhere less insane."

She sighed, pressing her cheek against the glass, then jumped when her door suddenly swung open. Neve whirled quickly, as if to block the view of the bear from whoever was coming in.

But nobody did.

"Hello?" She crossed the room and peered out the door into the dimly lit hallway. "Hello?"

No one was there. No orderlies. No nurses. Nothing.

Then she heard a loud click off to the left, followed by the unmistakable creak of a door opening.

*Could this place get any weirder?*

Neve glanced back at the bear, who now sat on his haunches, waiting for her.

"I'll be right back," she whispered, feeling silly, but as if she shouldn't leave it waiting. She poked her head into the hallway and heard another low creak. Neve moved quietly, following the sound, and turned the corner to find an emergency exit standing wide open. The sign beside it clearly read *Alarm will sound if door is opened.*

"Must be broken," she murmured, inching toward the opening. She peeked out at the empty courtyard and could see the bear still sitting by her window.

She jerked away from the door. "Okay, let's think this through," she whispered. "You're in here. A big scary bear is out there. You're going to stay in here, right?"

But . . . once she got past the sheer size of it, the bear really didn't seem that scary. She snuck another quick look outside. The bear was idly scratching his ear, yawning widely.

Man, it had a huge mouth. But Neve still had a feeling that it was . . . well, if not *friendly* exactly, that it didn't want to hurt her.

Why did it keep coming to her window? Why

did it seem to be *looking* for her?

"Ugh. You're crazy, you know?" she mumbled to herself, but she stepped through the door, leaving it open a crack behind her. The bear's ears perked up and it turned toward her, getting to its feet.

"Okay, big fellow," she said, taking one step forward. "We're going to take this really slow, okay? And you're not going to eat me, right?"

The bear snorted, as if it understood her words.

"Do bears eat people?" she asked, taking another step, but keeping the door in her peripheral vision. "I thought it was mostly salmon and berries, or whatever. You do maim people, though, right? So, no maiming. Please."

The bear sat down again, still staring at her. She moved closer, but it kept perfectly still.

"I can't believe this is happening," she said when a mere three feet of space lay between them.

The bear didn't move.

She inched closer, swallowing thickly, then slowly reached out. Would it let her touch it? Would it bite her hand off?

The click of a lock and rattle of a doorknob jerked them both out of the stillness and the bear raced toward the woods before Neve even realized what was happening.

"Hey—"

One of the french doors to the common room swung open, and Neve jumped into the shadows, panicked. She melted into the exterior wall, gripping onto the groove between panels of siding.

"Don't see me. Don't see me. Don't see me," she chanted silently as Calum walked out into the yard. Her eyes darted to the emergency exit door, but there was no way she could make it without him spotting her.

*Don't see me. Don't see me. Don't see me.*

He wandered onto the path, scanning the edge of the forest as he puffed on a cigarette. He came to a stop directly across the lawn from where Neve stood, frozen, his back to her as he stared into the trees. Then, with a flick of ash onto the ground, he turned around to look right at her.

She held her breath. Was she hidden enough in the shadows?

*Don't see me. Don't see me. Don't see me.*

His head turned in a wide arc as he took another puff from his cigarette, but his gaze skipped right over her, as if she weren't there. Then, dropping the butt onto the ground, he snuffed it out with the heel of his sneaker before heading back inside.

It wasn't until the door closed and a good thirty seconds had passed that Neve was able to get her shaking legs to carry her back through the emergency exit door, down the hall, and into her own room.

She closed the door quietly, then rushed to the

window, pushing the curtains open wider and frantically searching for the bear. It was only then that a flashing shimmer caught her attention and she noticed the sleeve of her sweatshirt had slipped up to show the fading lines of the snowflake tattoo.

Her mind raced. There was a connection there . . . between the bear and the tattoo, and —

Neve looked at the spot where she'd been standing earlier, where Calum hadn't seen her. She'd thought she'd been hidden by the shadows, but now that she examined it more closely, she saw the area was dimly lit by the lamp post on the corner. Even in the darkness, Calum should have seen her. There was no way he could have *missed* her.

But he had.

Slowly, strange keys started to fit into bizarre locks. The thoughts made no sense, but they ran through her head anyway.

She'd wanted to go outside, and the doors had opened. Wanted Calum not to see her, and he hadn't.

It was like . . . magic. Almost as if she'd wished for things to happen, and the wishes had come true.

Neve traced a finger over the spot where she'd seen the snowflake glittering on her skin. Could it all be connected somehow? The bear. The tattoo. The sparks that burned when she was upset. The bear that behaved as no bear should?

What did it all mean? She felt as if she had the answer on the tip of her tongue . . . that it was around the corner, waiting for her to discover it, but kept slipping away right as she was about to grab it.

Neve had no idea how long she stood there at the window, lost in thought and watching . . . hoping that the bear might reappear. But after a while, exhaustion claimed her, and she climbed back into bed and fell into a deep, dreamless sleep.

Hours later, the bear stood alert in the shadows, hidden by the trees but with the girl's window in clear sight. He had no words for what he was doing, of course. He was a bear, after all. But he knew he needed to always be on watch. To make sure she was safe.

To protect her.

It was his only mission. An instinct that overrode all others.

His gaze never leaving the building, he leaned over to bite at a bit of fungus growing on a nearby tree. The sun would rise soon, and he would have to abandon his post, but he wouldn't leave until the last possible moment.

A familiar scent caught his attention, and he

growled low in his throat as the creature came into view, bypassing the window with a click of its tongue.

A rage so deep, so raw that it nearly ate him up from the inside filled the bear, only compounded by its inability to lunge, to rip the creature's throat wide open and leave it bleeding on the ground. Unable to roar, he fought against the invisible bonds, but he wasn't strong enough to break them.

The creature only laughed as it approached his hiding place, ducking its head to peer at the bear in open mockery.

"There's really no need for you to keep watch, you know," it said, shaking its head. "I have no desire to harm the girl. That would kind of defeat the purpose, wouldn't it?"

The bear flashed its teeth, claws curling into the damp ground in frustration.

"But do as you will. It will make no difference in the end." Its smile turned vicious. "I'm close, you know. Very close." He straightened and glanced at the sky.

"Time's running out." The creature turned then, not afraid at all of the furious wild animal at its back. It strolled back into the building, leaving the bear all but frothing at the mouth.

But a movement in the window caught his attention, distracting him from his fury. The girl had opened the curtains and stood looking out. She couldn't see him yet, not in the weak light of predawn, but he dared not step into the open, not when his sharp hearing told him so many were already beginning to stir.

She yawned and rubbed at her eyes, then looked down at her inner arm for a moment, tracing the skin there with her other hand. The bear had a strong urge to go to her, to lead her away and bring her somewhere safe. Somewhere he could protect her.

But he couldn't, of course. This was all he could do.

Watch and wait.

After a while, the girl turned and left the window and the bear glanced up at the lightening sky. The sun would break the horizon soon, so his watch was almost over. He could feel it itching under his fur, throbbing in his heart.

He took one last look at the window before the first pink streams of dawn lit the sky, then abandoned his post until nightfall.

He would not fail her.

Not again.

# Chapter Six

Now that Neve had her eyes opened to the weirdness around her, she found more of it everywhere she looked. Lily continued to keep her distance with a wary eye, hastily stuffing her mouth with food and leaving the common room whenever Neve entered. Tala ignored everyone, including Torbin, although he made no effort to go near her, either.

And they weren't the only patients who were acting strange. Nancy went missing for a few days then showed up at group without her ever-present crochet hook. Peter, who'd always dominated any conversation, became quiet and withdrawn, barely speaking, even when asked a direct question.

In fact, it seemed like pretty much every patient disappeared for so-called *intensive individual therapy* for days at a time and would return haggard and drawn with shuffling feet and bowed shoulders.

Whatever this intensive therapy was, it definitely didn't seem to have a positive effect. Neve wondered how long she'd be able to avoid it, and tried to stay under the radar as much as possible, observing quietly and keeping up an appearance of acquiescence.

Appearances, however, could be very deceiving.

She'd become convinced that the staff at Blackbriar definitely did not have the best interests of its patients at heart, but she wasn't sure yet what to do about it. It wasn't as though Neve could simply walk away. Cameras kept tabs on all of them at every moment, and she knew any attempt to leave would mean a return of the restraints and the drugs, and she couldn't risk it.

Not until she figured out exactly what was happening.

She'd started to have flashes of memories — vague, hazy things she first attributed to delusion until she realized she couldn't interact with them like she could with Rose. The longer she went without the meds, the clearer the images became — a russet horse running across a green pasture, laundry hanging on a line, something simmering in an iron pot on a stove. Mundane, everyday things at first, then images that crept into the fantastical: her own sparkling hands holding another person's, the intertwined fingers shimmering with electric power, her own feet floating above the earth as she looked down with glee . . . a candle bursting into flame without a match in sight.

None of it made sense. None of it was logical.

But she was convinced that the medication that Doctor Alberich had prescribed had nothing to do with making her better. Instead, she suspected it did the opposite. That it repressed her memories somehow, and now that it was being flushed out of her system, they were beginning to return.

Neve figured her memory was like a muscle that needed retraining. So, she'd spend hours focusing on a certain memory, trying to pinpoint minute details and how she was feeling at a particular moment. It seemed to work, although she was careful to keep her progress to herself.

*Don't trust him.* That definitely extended to the entire staff at Blackbriar now, including Doctor Alberich.

She'd also been trying to recreate the emotions leading to the sparks and the shimmering tattoo, although she hadn't had much luck with that, yet. As for the wishes?

Well, she'd had a little progress on that front, at least.

One afternoon, almost three weeks since she first awoke at Blackbriar, Neve sat on a bench during free time, watching a group playing croquet, while a few others walked circuits around the lawn for exercise. Torbin loomed nearby, as usual, and Lily and Tala were nowhere to be seen.

Nancy lined up for her shot, missing the wicket entirely as the red ball rolled toward the edge of the path, and Neve sat up a little straighter, seeing an opportunity. She'd found her *wishes* worked best when she did what she'd done the night with the bear.

*Don't see it. Don't see it. Don't see it.* She chanted over and over in her head, focused solely on Nancy, who walked over in search of the ball. The woman looked down at the grass, her brow creased in confusion.

"Where did it go?" she called back to the group.

"It's right there," Peter replied, lining up his own shot. "Next to your foot."

*Don't see it. Don't see it. Don't see it.*

Nancy turned in a circle, staring down at the ground, but even though she barely missed kicking the ball with the side of her foot, she made no indication that she saw it at all.

Neve let her concentration ease, and Nancy blinked down at the ground.

"Oh, there it is," she said, bending to pick it up. "If it was a snake, it would have bit me." She rejoined the game without another thought, and Neve smiled in satisfaction.

She couldn't explain it, but that was a trick she

felt would definitely prove useful. On a victory high, she stood and walked slowly over toward Torbin, sending a *Don't see me* back at Angelica, who stood near the french doors, keeping watch.

"I need to talk to you," Neve told him.

He cocked a brow in response.

"Tala wasn't at breakfast," she said. "Has she been taken for *therapy*?" She used air quotes to indicate exactly what she thought of the idea.

Torbin's whole body tightened, and when he gave a slight nod, it was as if it took all his effort.

"We need to find her," Neve said. "Have you noticed how sick everyone looks when they get done with one of those therapy sessions? I mean, look at Nancy." She pointed toward the croquet game, noting that Angelica was still not looking in their direction. *Good. Don't see me.*

"It looks like she's aged ten years." Neve lowered her voice, just in case. "Same with Peter and Lily. Like they've had the life sucked right out of them."

Torbin frowned, shooting a quick glance toward Angelica.

"I know they're watching," she replied with a frustrated groan. "But you know the camera dead spots, right?"

He nodded.

"Is there a way to get around the Institute without being spotted?"

He hesitated, then nodded again before looking pointedly toward Angelica one more time.

"I think I can handle them," she said with a slight smile. "I seem to have the power of invisibility."

Torbin stared at her, unblinking.

"Okay, not *invisibility* per se, but—" She chewed on her lip, then looked him in the eye. "I know this sounds crazy, but I—somehow—can make people not see me. I don't know if I'm messing with their eyes or their mind or what, but—" When he gave no response, she huffed.

"Okay, look." She turned around and thought for a moment. "I'm not sure this will work. I've never tried it with more than one person, but—" She closed her eyes, focusing her thoughts, then opened them slowly.

*Don't see us. Don't see us. Don't see us.*

And with that, she took off at a dead run for the path in the forest.

A moment later, she heard Torbin chase after her, but as far as she could tell, nobody else noticed what she was doing. She raced down the path, sneakers slapping against the soft ground, and only stopped when she could no longer hear voices or the click of croquet balls.

Neve turned to face Torbin, a victorious smile on her face. "See?" she said through heavy breaths.

She needed to get in better shape.

Torbin's brow furrowed as he studied her, turning his head back toward the path, then facing her again deliberately.

"I know, it's awesome right?" she said. "I don't know how I'm doing it. I mean, who can *do* that? It's like something from a movie."

Then the most amazing thing happened. Torbin's face, so stoic and hard, broke into a wide, happy smile.

It stunned Neve, abruptly stopping her steady stream of words. The sharp creases in his face vanished, except for the curves around his lips, and his dark eyes sparkled. She took a moment to appreciate his thick lashes, the sharp line of his jaw, sprinkled with stubble . . . the fullness of his lower lip where his teeth —

She shuddered, then swallowed nervously.

Sure, Torbin was handsome. Even when she was pretty sure he hated her, she could have admitted that. But when he smiled his whole face — his whole *body* lit up, and the effect was mesmerizing.

He stepped closer to her, and her breath caught as her heart hammered in her chest. He reached out, and she thought for a moment he was going to stroke her cheek or maybe tip her chin up so he could —

Torbin tapped her forehead with one finger, a

questioning look on his face.

"What?" she asked in a raspy voice. Clearing her throat, she tried again. "What?"

He tapped her forehead.

"My head?" she asked, still a little dazed. "My brain?"

He nodded. *Yes.*

"You want to know about my brain?" Neve frowned in confusion, until it clicked. "My memories?"

A more enthusiastic nod. *Yes.*

"I think they're coming back," she replied. "It's the medication, right? That's why you told me to stop taking it?"

*Yes.*

"I knew it." She held up a finger, shaking it at him. "It's Doctor Alberich, right? That guy can't be trusted."

To her surprise, there was no nod. Only a general tightening of Torbin's muscles, from his pulsing jaw to his clenched fists. He held painfully still, solid and unmoving.

"It doesn't matter. Not right now, anyway. It's okay." For the first time, Neve reached out and touched Torbin, wrapping her fingers around his thick wrist. He froze at the touch, his warm brown gaze meeting hers. Neve swallowed, and slowly released him, wiping her now damp palm against her sweatpants.

Torbin looked away for a moment, then straightened and grabbed each of his wrists, one after the other. His sign for Tala.

"We need to find her," Neve said, concern thickening her voice. "Will you help me?"

Torbin's whole body went rigid, his eyes fierce, and he nodded.

Despite her determination to find Tala, Neve wasn't sure exactly how they would manage it. Torbin, however, convinced her in his yes-or-no-questions way that he had an idea. She followed him out of the forest, reinforcing what she'd come to think of as her concealment chant as they emerged onto the lawn.

No one even glanced in their direction, and Neve realized it was getting easier to avoid detection. It still took a lot of focus, especially when targeting a group of people, rather than only one, but it was becoming more . . . *natural*, she supposed. Like she could slip into the mental space with a little less effort.

It excited her to think that she might be able to strengthen that ability like she did her memories.

Instead of heading to the french doors, Torbin led her around the opposite corner of the building to a set of concrete steps partially hidden by a low hedge. With a quick glance around, he went down the stairs, pausing at the gray metal door at the bottom. She could tell when he tried to turn the doorknob that it was locked, but he wrenched it hard, biceps bulging, and the knob gave way with a harsh crunch. He swung the door open and jerked his head toward the opening for her to precede him.

"Won't they notice that?" she whispered, eyeing the broken lock.

He simply pulled the door shut firmly and shrugged before pressing a finger to his lips and leading her down a narrow, dimly lit hallway. The walls were concrete block with peeling paint, the floor thick, yellowed linoleum with spidery cracks every few feet. No windows, only the flicker of a row of fluorescent lights overhead. They passed a few closed doors before coming to a stop at the corner, and Torbin pressed her back against the damp wall with a firm hand on her shoulder. After a moment, he tugged her along, moving quickly across the hall to huddle next to an open doorway. Torbin had positioned her between him and the door, and he jerked his head toward the opening, widening his dark eyes to emphasize the movement.

She edged closer to the doorway and took a quick peek into the room. A man sat with his back to them, watching a bank of television monitors. Evidently, the security cameras from the whole

Institute fed into this one room.

Monitored by this one person.

Torbin nudged her, an expectant expression on his face.

Could she do it? There was only one way to find out. She closed her eyes and focused on the man in the office.

*Don't see us. Don't see us.*

She took a breath and looked up, scanning the hall ceiling until she spotted a camera about fifty feet down, next to another stairway. With one last, fervent *Don't see us* mentally chanted toward the security guard, she dashed down the hall with Torbin. They passed under the camera and stood against the wall directly beneath it, waiting. After a few moments, when nobody sounded an alarm, they grinned at each other triumphantly.

It worked.

Once they got a little farther from the office, Neve thought it safe enough to ask, "I didn't even know this was down here. Do you think this is where they have Tala?"

Torbin said nothing but led her down another hallway.

"Shouldn't we check those doors we passed on the way in?"

He shook his head. She guessed this wasn't the first time he'd explored the basement, although he must not have been able to get too far. Regardless, he moved with assurance now, as if he completely trusted whatever she was doing to protect them.

They turned another corner and, one by one, he started opening doors. Neve took the other side of the hallway, keeping her concealment chant going in a quiet rhythm. Neve had thought the further she got from the security guard, the more difficult it would be, but it was actually like there was a mental tether between the two of them. Like once the link was established, keeping up the gentle patter of suggestion was almost subconscious.

She followed Torbin's lead, pressing an ear to each door to listen for movement inside before quietly opening it. She found storage rooms and what appeared to have once been an office, the desk, chair, and filing cabinet thick with dust. But there was no sign of treatment rooms, no medical equipment, no nurses, and no sign of any patients.

They neared a set of swinging doors at the end of the hall and a frisson of awareness ran up Neve's spine. Call it instinct or a gut feeling, but she knew somehow, they were on the right track. She started to push through the doors, but Torbin held up a hand to stop her, peering through a small, square window at the top of the door before he nodded once.

The silence was unnerving, but it was more than that. The further they descended into the depths of the basement, the more uneasy Neve became. It was as if something was telling her this place was bad . . . wrong. It made her skin itch, her stomach twist . . . her palms grow slippery with sweat. She swiped them on her thighs and drew an unsteady breath.

The door creaked as it swung on its hinges, raising goosebumps along Neve's arms. They crept into a wider hallway with a half-dozen closed doors, all with plastic pockets mounted below windows crisscrossed with wire mesh. She and Torbin exchanged a weighted glance.

They were in the right place.

The windows were too high for her to see through, but Torbin checked every one, shaking his head to indicate they were empty. One door at the end of the hall stood open and she could spot a hospital bed, ceiling mounted curtains shoved to the wall, and a couple medical monitors. To her surprise, half-melted candles circled the bed, puddled wax hardened on the worn linoleum.

"What were they doing in here?" she murmured, half to herself.

Torbin inhaled sharply and grimaced as if he smelled something bad, growling low in his throat.

Neve sniffed, but couldn't smell anything other than the same damp, mildewy odor that seemed to permeate the entire basement. They'd reached the end of the hallway where it T'd off to both sides, and Neve looked first right, then left.

"Which way?" she whispered.

Then, she heard it—at the same time as Torbin, if the jerk of his head was any indication—the slow, unmistakable beeping of a heart monitor.

Together, they turned to the left, following the sound.

It was odd that there was no staff around. Neve figured they must assume no one would ever venture down to the obviously forbidden area. She decided to be thankful for small favors, glad she didn't have to split her concentration. The link with the security guard seemed stable, and still appeared to be working, she thought with relief as they passed under another camera.

The beeping grew louder and, without thinking, Neve reached for Torbin's hand. He made no response other than to give her a gentle squeeze of reassurance. It surprised Neve a little how the simple touch calmed her, how the press of his palm against hers steadied her, a reassurance that she wasn't alone.

It was bizarre, if she thought about it. When she first saw Torbin, she'd thought he hated her. Now, he was pretty much the only one at Blackbriar she could count on.

Could *trust*.

They came to a room at the end of the hall and, after checking the window, Torbin opened the door. The monitor beeps emanated from behind a hospital curtain in the far corner of the room. The area outside the curtain was completely empty, except for a broken folding chair leaning against the wall.

Torbin flicked on the overhead light and it buzzed, casting the room in a sickly yellowish glow. The beeping remained steady, accented by the quiet whoosh of an automated blood pressure cuff. He stood still, head tilted as he listened for a moment, then he pulled the curtain aside.

Tala lay sleeping on the hospital bed, an oxygen cannula curled under her nose and over her ears. She had an I.V. needle in the back on one hand, the blood pressure cuff around the opposite arm. A variety of wires wound around her, some slipping beneath the faded hospital gown she wore, others clipped to two square pads at her temples. As in the room Neve had seen earlier, candles surrounded the bed, although these were brand new and unlit. Tala's leather bracelets had been tossed on a small table near the head of the bed, next to a collection of bottles filled with fluids in various color and a large geode, nearly the size of a football, bursting with sparkling black crystals.

"What are they doing to her?" Neve drew closer to the bed, opposite Torbin. He shook Tala's shoulder as if to wake her.

She didn't move. Her eyelids didn't flutter, and her heart rate remained slow and steady.

Neve leaned in and whispered, "Tala?" Then, a

little louder, "Tala, wake up."

Nothing.

"They must have her sedated." Neve eyed the I.V. bag. "Do you think we can—"

With no warning, Tala shot up and screamed at the top of her lungs. Her eyes were wild as she clawed at her chest, ripping the wires from her skin. She yanked at the I.V. needle and blood trickled from the puncture point.

"Tala, stop." Neve reached out to catch her wrists and calm her as Torbin grabbed her face, trying to meet her gaze. But it was as if she didn't see either of them. The screams lessened to quiet whimpers, then, like air let out of a balloon, she collapsed back onto the bed, unconscious.

"What in the world—" Neve's own heart was pounding, her breath coming in harsh pants.

Then an alarm sounded on the heart rate monitor, and she cursed under her breath.

"Someone's going to hear that," she hissed at Torbin. "We have to go. Now."

He shook his head and reached for Tala, slipping his arms under her back and legs.

"You can't," she said, reaching across the bed to grip his arm. "If she disappears, they'll come looking for her. And where are we going to hide her?"

He let out a frustrated breath.

"I know." Neve gritted her own teeth. "I don't

want to leave her either, but we need a plan. We can't run off with her. They'll catch us and drug us both and lock us up. Then we won't be able to do anybody any good."

He hesitated, then stiffened at the sound of approaching footsteps.

"Torbin, we have to go," Neve whispered. "We'll come back for her. I promise."

His jaw tightened but he gave a sharp nod. They huddled in the corner near the door as the security guard came into the room, and Neve reestablished her link to him, hiding them from his view.

They slipped out as he reconnected the loose wires, mumbling in irritation, and retraced their steps at a run. Neve only let out a relieved breath once they'd made it outside.

Torbin looked murderous. He stalked toward the lawn, but froze when Neve grabbed his elbow.

"We'll go back for her," she said.

He huffed, but nodded.

"But I don't know where we'll even go once we do," she continued, starting to pace. "We need to get out of here. It's pretty obvious that Blackbriar is not what it claims to be."

Torbin waited expectantly.

"Do you know what's out there?" she asked, waving to the surrounding forest. "Can we get out that way?"

He frowned, then shook his head, slapping a hand against the brick wall.

"A wall?" she asked. "Around the whole thing?"

He nodded.

"So, the only way out is the main entrance. Not that I've seen it, but there's got to be one." Torbin nodded as she paced a bit and thought out loud. "And they're not going to let us walk out the front door."

Torbin pointed to her forehead, then mimed covering his eyes.

"Hide us?" She laughed. "I'm not sure I can. Not yet."

At his confused look, she added. "I'm not only talking about the three of us, Torbin. We *all* need to get out of here."

He glanced toward the sounds of laughter and shouts from the courtyard, then back at Neve, wide-eyed.

*All of us?*

"Whatever's going on here. Whatever Doctor Alberich is up to? He's doing it to everybody," she said. "We can't leave anyone behind."

Torbin shook his head, jabbing a finger toward the basement door, then at Neve, then off to the side.

*We need to go!*

"I know!" Neve threw up her hands. "Look,"

she said, "my . . . ability, for lack of a better word, seems to be getting stronger. When we came out of the forest, I was able to hide us from a big group. I'd never done that before. And in the basement? I had a kind of connection to the security guard which enabled me to keep us hidden without having to concentrate too hard. I think—" She crossed her arms and chewed on her fingernail. "I think I can do it. Hide us all. But I need to try it out first. Practice."

Torbin tapped an invisible wristwatch on the back of his hand.

*How long?*

"I don't know," she admitted. "But I will do my best. I'll work on it. I promise. In the meantime, it would be nice if we could cause a distraction or something. Keep Doctor Alberich occupied so he doesn't have time to do whatever he's doing to Tala?"

Torbin's eyes narrowed, then a slow, evil smile spread over his face.

Neve arched a brow. "I take it you have an idea?"

Torbin nodded and pounded a fist on his chest.

*Leave it to me.*

# CHAPTER SEVEN

From that moment on, Neve spent as much time as she could honing her skills. She'd practice hiding herself from large groups . . . hiding large groups from others.

Hiding people. Hiding things.

Honing in on the tether she'd felt in the basement. Exploring it . . . stretching it and reeling it in. Over the next week, she got to know her gift and soon it was responding almost instantaneously.

But that was only the beginning.

The evening after they'd found Tala, Neve had been sitting on her bed, practicing. There was no one to practice *on* really, but she reached out with her tether and found she could connect with different people, and even recognize them by their link. Calum's felt tight, electric, but Angelica's was looser and more elastic. She was pondering what that could mean when lightning flashed through her window, followed by the sharp crack of thunder. Neve got up and approached the window. She hadn't noticed while she'd been concentrating, but the sky had grown dark with nearly black clouds roiling across the sky. She could feel the electricity in the air, static crackling across her skin.

Rain started to fall, a light pitter pat at first, but quickly building to a torrential downpour. It pounded on the gravel walk, bent the flowers under its unrelenting drive. Another flash of lightning made her jump, her hand flying to her mouth in surprise.

Then, she saw it. Colorful sparkles dancing across her fingertips.

In awe, Neve turned her hands over and back again, watching the sparks move along her skin. Now that she was paying attention, she noticed the electric warmth running up and down her arms. The lightning flashed again, and the sparks brightened, expanding for a second before returning to their earlier size.

"Weird," she murmured, her gaze drifting from her hands to the sky and back again.

Could there—could there be a connection?

As if answering her question, the sky lit again with another bolt of lightning—closer this time—and the sparks brightened even more. An astonished laugh burst out of her and she closed her eyes, searching for that connection.

Could it be a tether like the one she used to hide things?

And just like that, a clarity hit her, as if her connection to the sparks had been hidden behind a curtain, waiting for her to pull it back. It w*as* a tether, a connection she felt not only to the lightning, but to the rain and the wind as well.

She flexed her fingers, and a tiny bolt of lightning flew from one index finger to the other.

"No way," she whispered, repeating the action.

Neve wanted to go outside, to truly test this newfound power, but a shriek outside her door had her running for the hallway. Nancy ran by her, screaming bloody murder, and soon the halls were full of patients.

"What's going on?" she asked Peter as he raced past.

"Rats!" he shouted with a shudder. "The place is full of rats!"

Neve watched the patients run this way and that, then spotted Torbin at the end of the hall, leaning against the wall with his beefy arms crossed over his chest and a satisfied smirk on his face. He caught her eye and winked.

Torbin . . . *Winked.*

Neve's cheeks heated, and a flutter of butterflies took flight in her stomach. She looked away quickly, embarrassed at her reaction.

What in the world was that?

She shook it off, taking in the mayhem around her. Nurses and orderlies were trying to corral the panicked patients, and she could hear Doctor Alberich shouting in the common room for someone to "Catch the one in the flour, for heaven's sake!"

True to his word, Torbin had caused a whopper of a diversion, and he seemed to be pretty proud of that fact.

The rats wreaked havoc for days. Doctor Alberich was definitely kept occupied organizing the orderlies to trap the vermin. It was interesting he chose not to call in an exterminator. As if he wanted no outsiders inside the gates.

Once the rats had been dealt with, a water leak flooded the library . . . then there was a small fire in one of the storage rooms.

Torbin kept the staff busy, and the doctor out of the basement.

Neve used the time to practice, a frantic edge to her training as she felt a ticking clock marking every passing second. The diversions would only work for so long, and the conviction that they were all in danger grew until it was all she could think about. More and more frequently, she found herself having to breathe deeply to calm down so she could focus enough to exercise her gifts, only to have panic rear up again as she thought of the challenges ahead.

Neve snuck down to the basement to check on Tala frequently and make sure she was all right. She seemed . . . the same. The candles were unlit, the bottles unmoved. The monitors continued to beep away, but for the time being, Tala appeared to be resting comfortably.

Early on the fifth day, however, Neve found the lock on the basement door had been repaired, and knew they were running out of time.

"It has to be tonight," she told Torbin as they stood at the edge of the forest during free time. "I think I'm ready."

Torbin nodded, then jerked his head toward the large group of patients playing ultimate Frisbee on the lawn.

"Wondering how we'll get them all to leave?" When Torbin nodded, she studied them, brow furrowed. "I don't know, to be honest. I'll have to convince them somehow, let them know they're in danger and we all have to get out."

Torbin looked skeptical. He scratched the scruff on his cheek, then pointed to her, to himself, and back toward the basement door.

"We can't leave them here!"

He mimed making a phone call.

"We have no way of knowing how long it would take before we could even find a phone to call for help," she replied, fighting to keep her voice down. "I don't know where we are, do you?"

A sharp huff. *No.*

"It could take days for us to find someone," she said. "And who knows what might happen to them if we left. They could move everyone. Or worse." She didn't like to think of worse. Worse was not even worth considering.

Torbin crossed his beefy arms and lifted his chin. He didn't like this. Not one bit.

"I know it's not going to be easy, but I don't have a choice, do I? It's not like *you* can talk them into it."

Torbin rolled his eyes, then pounded a fist into the opposite palm.

"I don't think threats are the way to go," she said. "I'll figure it out. Trust me."

Torbin gave her a long look, then his eyes softened ever-so-slightly, and he dipped his chin in a nod.

"Thanks," she said. "I'll be in touch."

Neve walked away from him, lifting the concealment as she joined a line of patients waiting to reenter the building. She wasn't sure how she would convince anyone that she wasn't crazy herself, let alone that they should trust her to help them escape a mental hospital where they all believed they should be in the first place.

But she *had* to figure out a way. There was no question about that.

Neve was starting to believe that all of their

lives depended on it.

"You seem distracted today, Neve." Doctor Alberich scribbled something in his ever-present notebook, drawing her out of her thoughts. It was her regular one-on-one therapy appointment, and they were sitting in a pair of leather chairs in the library. Doctor Alberich preferred to see patients either in the library or the garden. As a matter of fact, Neve didn't think anyone even knew where his office was.

The leather squeaked as she shifted in her chair. "Sorry, doctor. I guess I've got a lot on my mind."

Nothing she wanted to tell *him* about, but Neve knew she needed to be more careful. If he grew suspicious of her, everything could fall apart.

"Oh?" He peered at her over the top of his glasses. "Anything you'd care to share?"

Neve swallowed, thinking fast. "I, uh, I guess I was thinking about my delusions," she said, wringing her hands a little to sell the portrayal of an anxious, submissive patient. "I haven't had one in a long time. And I guess I was wondering, uh, how long you think I'll need to stay here?" She gave him what she hoped came across as a hopeful look.

He smiled slightly but shook his head. "Oh,

Neve," he said, condescension dripping from his voice. "I know you want to get better. We all want that. But I'm afraid you still have a way to go." He uncrossed and recrossed his legs. "We have control of the delusions, but there's still the matter of the amnesia. You haven't regained any memories, have you?" His black eyes narrowed, beady and piercing, and she tried not to fidget under his stare.

"No, nothing," she lied. "I don't remember anything before waking up here." She slipped a hand into the pocket of her sweatpants and pinched her thigh, hard. Tears formed in her eyes, and she let her voice go quavery. "I'm beginning to wonder if I'll ever remember." She sat up quickly. "Can you—can you tell me anything about myself? Even something small? Maybe that would help."

"Neve, we've talked about this—"

"I know you want me to do it on my own, but it's not happening," she said. This was dangerous. She knew it was dangerous, but she couldn't resist.

"Maybe the special individual therapy you do with some of the patients?" she asked. "Like Lily and Tala?" She watched him closely to gauge his reaction, but the guy was good. Stoic and unmoving.

"I'm afraid you're not quite ready for that yet," he said. "But Neve, you'll get there. I promise." He glanced at the clock on the wall. "I think that's our time for now. Please, don't rush things, all right,

Neve? It'll come. Just follow the program, take your meds, and everything will be okay."

She swallowed and tried to look meek, hiding the anger inside. "Yes, Doctor. I will."

"All right, then. I'll see you later." He focused on his notebook, effectively dismissing her, and she left the room, a distasteful shiver running down her spine.

The guy acted like he cared about them, had their best interests at heart . . . wanted them to get *better.* But all the while he was doing some kind of weird experiments on his patients. That had to be it. He was trying out some new, unapproved medication or treatment and using all of them as guinea pigs.

Well, not *all* of them. Apparently, Neve wasn't quite ready. Although she didn't know how ready you had to be for what Tala was going through.

She gave herself a little shake. There wasn't time to think about whatever Doctor Alberich was up to. She needed to focus on the job at hand.

Instead of going to her room to practice, as had become her habit, Neve made her way to the common room. A few patients were scattered around the room, some reading, some playing board games. Lily was putting together a puzzle with the teenager, Alice.

Where to begin?

She spotted Melissa from group in the corner,

drawing on a notepad in long, even strokes. She looked up as Neve approached, but back down quickly, hunching over her pad, her long dark hair hiding her face.

"Hi, Melissa," Neve said brightly. "How are you?"

The woman glanced up through her hair briefly. "Fine."

"Uh." Neve licked her lips, then dragged a chair over. "Mind if I sit here?"

Melissa gave her a confused look. "I . . . guess?"

"Great!"

Okay, so this was going to be tougher than she thought. Neve plucked a book from a shelf near her elbow and flipped it open, eyeing Melissa over the top of it. After a few moments, she dropped the book to her lap. "What are you drawing?"

Melissa hesitated for a moment, before turning the pad so Neve could see. It was a charcoal drawing of a waterfall, and although the lines were rough, the colors monotone, even Neve could see the talent at work. The water really looked like it was moving, crashing over the rocks below. Trees shaded a large pool at the bottom of the falls, and someone stood behind the wall of water, as if in a cave.

"Wow, that's . . . amazing, Melissa. You're really talented."

The woman ducked her head and blushed. "Thanks."

"Is that a real place?" she asked. "Or something you imagined?"

Melissa, to Neve's surprise, snorted lightly. "Who can tell anymore."

And Neve knew exactly what she meant. Reality and illusion kind of blended in her own life, after all. It hadn't occurred to her that it could be the same for others.

She scooted her chair a little closer. "Melissa, can I ask you something?"

The woman nodded but went back to her drawing.

"How long have you been here?"

Melissa lay the pad on her lap and looked toward the ceiling, thinking. "About a year, I guess."

"And do you—" Neve glanced over her shoulder to make sure no one was listening. "Do you think it's helping?"

She looked surprised at the question. "I think so."

"Don't you—" She swallowed. There was no time to beat around the bush. Best get to it. "Don't you think this place is kind of strange?"

"What do you mean?"

"I mean that people disappear for days at a time, then show up and are completely different.

Have you noticed that?"

She cut her eyes to the side. "Not really."

There was no other way. She had to come clean. "Melissa, did you know there's a basement to this place? That they're doing some kind of weird experiments down there?"

Melissa's shoulders curled up toward her ears. "I don't think we should be talking about this."

"No, I'm serious," Neve said, moving closer to her. "I saw what they're doing and it's not good, Melissa. We're all in danger."

"You shouldn't say that," Melissa said, her voice growing louder, a little frantic. "You shouldn't say those things!"

"Shh!" Neve fluttered her hands, trying to quiet her. "It's okay. We're going to help you."

"I think you should go now," Melissa said, jumping to her feet. Her notepad fell to the floor, and she clutched the charcoal in one white-knuckled fist. "I don't want to talk about this."

"But—"

"I don't want to!" she shouted, and every head turned toward them.

"Okay! Okay!" Neve got up and backed away, hands up defensively. "It's okay, Melissa. I'm sorry. I'm going."

Melissa stood, trembling for a moment, then picked up her notebook and started drawing again, as if the whole interaction had never happened.

Neve thought this might be more difficult than she'd anticipated.

Over the next hour or so, she tried again with a few other people, with similar, if a little less violent, results. It turned out everyone pretty much thought everyone else in Blackbriar was crazy, so Neve's claims were taken as the insane ramblings of, well, a mental patient.

It was when she was talking to Peter that she had an idea. The man was basically ignoring her as she told him about the basement and the experiments, and Neve let out a dejected sigh, staring at the top of his head as he flipped through a year-old car magazine.

She chewed on her lip with frustration, then narrowed her eyes and thought *believe me.*

*Believe me. Believe me. Believe me.*

Suddenly, he looked up, his eyes a bit vacant but a little frantic. "We need to get out of here."

Neve blinked. She hadn't really thought it would work. "We will."

"No, we have to get out of here now!" he shouted, jumping to his feet. "They're going to kill us!" he screamed.

"Peter, don't," Neve hissed at him. "Sit down. They'll hear you."

"Oh no!" Tears filled his eyes as he clamped his hands over his mouth. "They'll hear me, then

129

they'll kill me!"

"No, that's not going to happen."

"What am I going to do?" he moaned. "What am I going to do?"

Neve didn't know, but *she* did the only thing she could think of.

*Forget what I said. Forget it. Forget it!*

Peter stiffened, as if he'd been slapped in the face, then sat down and turned a page in the magazine.

Neve's hands were shaking. She couldn't believe what had just happened, couldn't believe that she'd actually *manipulated* someone like that. It made her feel ashamed, dirty . . . sick to her stomach.

She was so absorbed in her remorse that she didn't hear the rubber-soled footsteps coming her way, didn't realize Calum and Angelica had even noticed the interchange until they took her by each arm, pulling her to her feet.

"The doctor wants to see you," Calum said with a sneer, and Neve was too stunned to even try to argue.

They took Neve to her room, and her mind raced as she tried to think of what to do. She knew now that there was much more to her ability than simply being able to hide things. She could make people *do* things. *Believe* things. But with the cameras, and the staff wandering the halls, in addition to Calum and Angelica, she didn't think she had the power to deal with them all.

So she went along peacefully, sitting on the bed when directed, and waited.

After about five minutes, Doctor Alberich came into the room. He seemed a bit harried and distracted, hissing a quiet order at Angelica before turning to Neve.

"It seems, Neve, that you haven't been completely honest with me."

She tried to look confused when all she felt was panic. "What do you mean, Doctor?"

"*What do you mean, Doctor?*" he mimicked, and she knew all bets were off. "I mean," he said, "that you've been spreading vicious rumors among the residents here at Blackbriar. That you've been snooping around in restricted areas. And that you've been trying to organize an *escape*, of all things."

There was no point in denying it. "Well, they need to know what you're doing down in the basement," she all but snarled at him. "You're hurting people, not helping them. What is it, some kind of illegal drug trial? Black market organs?"

The doctor laughed. "You watch too many movies."

"What is it then?" she asked.

At that moment, the doctor's smile twisted into a grimace. "You're sick, Neve," he said. "We only want to help you."

Angelica walked into the room holding a hypodermic needle. She handed it to the doctor.

"This will make you feel better," he said, flicking the syringe with his finger before he pushed gently on the plunger until a drop of fluid escaped. "Push up your sleeve."

Neve did not want that medication. At all. She focused on Doctor Alberich's black eyes and pushed her thoughts at him as if she were shouting.

*Don't do it. Don't do it. Don't do it!*

He looked surprised for a second, then a slow smile lit his face. "Ah, so you do remember a few things," he said, and Neve's stomach twisted in fear.

He *knew*.

In a flash, he'd grabbed her arm in an iron grip and injected the drugs before she even realized what had happened. The room began to blur around the edges, and she couldn't resist when Angelica eased her back onto the bed.

She thought the doctor whispered something to her right before the blackness claimed her. She couldn't have been sure, of course, everything was a bit fuzzy and surreal. But she thought he leaned in with a wicked little smile and said, "Your little tricks won't work on me, witch."

It all seemed like a dream, though, and when she woke in the morning her body still felt heavy, her head muddled and thick. She tried to rub her bleary eyes, but she was tied down again, wrists and ankles in tight restraints. An I.V. had been set up near the bed, the needle piercing a vein on the back of her hand. She tried to read the label on the bag, but it was turned away from her.

"Great," she muttered. "Now what?"

The door clicked and she closed her eyes, evening out her breath as if she were still asleep.

"You sure you can do this?" Calum asked. "The doctor said he wanted to handle this personally."

Angelica laughed. "She's asleep. It's not like she's going to do anything." Neve could feel her move into the room and cracked her eyes to get a peek at what was coming. Angelica held another syringe in her hand and approached the I.V. bag. She injected the drugs into a port on the bag and turned back to Calum with a victorious smile.

"Told you," she said.

"Whatever," Calum muttered. "I've got other stuff to do."

He left the room, and Neve knew she didn't have much time. The drugs were easing into her system, her mind already starting to spin, but she'd explored the tether to Angelica many times before.

Although it was a little harder to access with her muzzy mind, once she was able to connect, it was strong and sure.

*Remove the I.V. needle.*

Angelica froze, her eyes going vacant.

*Remove the needle.*

She turned and peeled off the tape over the needle in the back of Neve's hand. She pulled it out and pressed a piece of gauze to the spot.

*Hide it.* Neve didn't even form words now, instead picturing what she wanted Angelica to do. Tape a piece of gauze down over the I.V. wound. Put the needle back, flat against the gauze. Tape it down so it looks like the needle is still in place.

Angelica did everything, then stood, blank-eyed as if waiting for instructions.

Neve considered her options, but it only took a moment to show her that there weren't many, at least not yet. She could get Angelica to release her, but then what? She still hadn't figured out how to escape with the other patients. And Alberich was on to her, so that was an added complication.

She couldn't influence him, for some reason. Maybe he had an exceptionally strong mind, or an ability of his own.

These were all things she needed to know if she was going to stop him.

As she had the thought, she realized the truth of it. It wasn't only about saving the patients at

Blackbriar, even more, it was about stopping Alberich. He couldn't be allowed to keep doing whatever he was doing. And if that meant she had to spend more time tied to a bed, so be it.

He thought he was in control, but Doctor Alberich better think again.

The doctor may have been able to resist Neve's influence, but he couldn't read her mind. Neve pretended to be unconscious, persuading Angelica or Calum or whoever was on duty to drain her I.V. bag in the sink periodically, so it looked like she was getting the medication. They brought her food, removed her restraints so she could relieve herself, and told the doctor the catheter was operating well.

All the while, Neve grew stronger.

It had been almost twenty-four hours, judging by the changing light through the windows, when the three of them came into her room, talking quietly.

"—should wear off soon. The last dose was four hours ago, correct?" Doctor Alberich asked.

"Yes, Doctor," Angelica replied.

"All right, it should be the same as last time," he said. "So look a little less threatening, Calum, if you please."

He huffed in exasperation. "I'm so tired of this."

"We all are," Doctor Alberich replied, "but we need her. She's the key to everything."

Neve fought hard not to react to that.

"But aren't we close enough?" Calum asked. "The last one—"

"No," the doctor snapped. "It's not ready. Not yet. We need to test it a few more times with the others first."

*Test it?* What in the world were they talking about?

Doctor Alberich let out a heavy breath. "Look, you both have been working very hard. Don't think I don't appreciate it. It's going to be soon. I promise. I'm very close to a breakthrough and then we'll all have everything we want. All right?"

There was no response, but Neve could only assume they agreed. She figured now was as good a time as any for the drugs she hadn't taken to wear off, so she shifted a little in the bed.

"Here she comes," Alberich said.

Neve opened her eyes, blinking a few times as if blinded by the overhead lights.

"It's all right, take your time," the doctor said. "We're all here to help you."

The words sparked a memory, and Neve realized he'd said the same thing the last time she woke up in Blackbriar with amnesia.

Doctor Alberich moved to the head of the bed and bent slightly over her, a gentle smile on his face.

"Do you know where you are?" he asked.

And she realized what the drugs were . . . what they were supposed to do.

"Do you know *who* you are?" Doctor Alberich asked.

Neve knew then what she had to say.

"Uh, Neve." She licked her lips, her brow wrinkled in confusion. "My name is Neve. But . . . where am I?"

# CHAPTER EIGHT

Talk about déjà vu all over again.

Neve wasn't sure she could pull it off, but Doctor Alberich seemed to believe that she'd lost her memory again. He played the patient healer, explaining her *condition* to her with a pitying smile . . . showing her the pictures of the girl in the medical file. He answered the same questions Neve had asked the first time she awoke, ordered Calum to remove the restraints with the same compassionate air.

Had he been so obviously lying the first time? Neve could now see the slight tightness at the corner of his mouth, the distaste in his fathomless eyes.

It was his overconfidence, she decided, that worked in her favor. He was so sure that his plan had worked that it never even occurred to him that it might not have. Neve wondered what was in the syringes that she'd convinced Angelica to empty into the toilet. Was there a drug that could cause amnesia?

Evidently so, and it looked like they were using it at Blackbriar on a regular basis.

Neve did the best she could to look lost and confused . . . to pretend not to recognize the common room or the yard, or the patients and staff walking the halls. Nobody spoke to her, she noticed, wondering if they'd all forgotten her as well, or if the doctor had some other technique for keeping Neve isolated.

She wondered where Torbin was. She hadn't seen him during the impromptu tour of Blackbriar and tried to be subtle while the doctor showed her the courtyard. She longed to search the shadows of the forest, though . . . to find him leaning against a tree, his arms crossed and the ever-present frown on his face.

He wasn't at group—nor was Tala—and Neve played innocent again as young Alice shyly introduced herself, followed by Nancy, Peter, and Melissa. Adam was gone, as well, though of course Neve couldn't ask about him. She sat silently listening as the others shared their thoughts and challenges and tried to hide the way her mind whirled with thoughts.

"Neve, would you like to share?" Doctor Alberich asked, and she pasted on a shy smile.

"Uh, I'm Neve," she said, then shook her head. "You probably know that. Do they know that?" she asked the doctor before waving a hand in dismissal. "Never mind. Anyway. I have amnesia and I guess delusions? So I, uh . . . " She shrugged. "I only want to get better."

The group clapped halfheartedly, and Doctor Alberich said, "That's very good, Neve. Thank you."

It was all she could do to keep from rolling her eyes.

But he moved on to someone else, and Neve entertained herself by seeing how far she could push Angelica. She couldn't practice her newfound abilities on the patients—that felt wrong—and Doctor Alberich was immune. Worse yet, he seemed to have been aware of what she was trying to do, like he could feel her poking around in his mind.

Calum and Angelica, however, were fair game. And pretty easy, to be perfectly honest.

Angelica sat on a folding chair near the door, behind Doctor Alberich, so he couldn't see what she was doing. Neve made it simple at first.

*Scratch your nose.*

Of course, it was tough to tell if she scratched it because Neve told her to, or because it itched. So Neve opted for something a little more unusual, sending a mental message for Angelica to cross and uncross her legs.

Several times.

If anyone had been paying attention, they might have found it odd that Angelica kept crossing and uncrossing her legs, but Neve smiled to herself, pleased with her progress.

But these were all parlor tricks, nothing that could help them in their endeavor to get the patients out and bring Blackbriar down. Could she get someone to buzz them through a locked security door? Turn off the cameras? Drive them out the gate?

Take one of those syringes and plunge it right into Doctor Alberich's neck?

She shuddered at the thought. Even though the man was definitely up to no good, Neve didn't know if she had it in her to go eye-for-an-eye at him. Then, she thought of Tala in that hospital bed . . . of Lily, shadow-eyed and haunted, and thought maybe, just maybe, she could.

Torbin was worried, and it was not an emotion he was accustomed to.

Anger? Yes.

Bitterness? Frustration? Absolutely.

He operated lately on a mix of resentment and

pure, black fury. But worry? No, that was something new. Because worry came from helplessness, and Torbin wasn't used to being helpless.

It was not part of his nature. Until recently.

He hadn't seen Neve since she'd told him she planned to bring everyone with them when they left Blackbriar. He thought it was ridiculous, of course. The smart plan was to simply leave and send help when they could.

Well, maybe kill Alberich on the way out. That would make it both smart *and* satisfying.

Still, it shouldn't have surprised him that Neve would want to save the others. It was a part of *her* nature, after all. But none of that mattered now because Neve was locked away in her room. Alberich had got wind of Neve's escape talk, and she'd been taken.

Every fiber of Torbin's being screamed to get to her—to rip the place apart until he did. But he couldn't, of course.

He was helpless. Powerless.

And thus, worried.

He stood in the shadow of a pine tree on the edge of the forest, the scent of the woods the only thing that kept him grounded. Around him, the others played games and exercised, but they gave him a wide berth. His black mood emanated off him like a shield, and they knew better than to get too close.

Torbin's teeth ground together when Alberich came out of the french doors. He walked casually, smiling as if he hadn't a care in the world, chatting and laughing and patting people on the back. It was all a show, of course.

Torbin wanted to rip his head off.

Alberich finally met his gaze, his lips twisting in a self-satisfied smirk as he drew nearer. He had to tip his head up to look at Torbin, but it didn't seem to bother him much that he was so much shorter. He simply propped his hands on his hips and shook his head slightly.

"Your little friend has been causing trouble," he said. "But I'm sure you'll be happy to know I put a stop to that."

Torbin tensed the muscles in his arms until they were tight and throbbing.

Alberich huffed out a humorless laugh. "She actually thought she could organize a little uprising, you know? A coup d'état? Did you have anything to do with that?"

Torbin couldn't respond, of course, other than to clench his jaw even tighter, hate burning in his eyes.

"No, of course not," Alberich said thoughtfully. "Not that it matters. She doesn't remember any of it now anyway. And she won't cause any more trouble. You won't either, will you." He deepened his voice on the last words, the sound vibrating through Torbin's body.

He shuddered, and his head dropped forward in defeat.

"Good."

At that moment, Torbin caught a flash of movement by the french doors and he drew a relieved breath when Neve walked out.

Alberich glanced over his shoulder and smiled. "Ah, yes, there's my prize patient," he said. "I should go make sure she has everything she needs." He shot a conniving grin at Torbin. "Wouldn't want her to get lonely."

Torbin seethed.

"You'd like to wrap those big hands around my neck, wouldn't you?" he murmured. "Squeeze until I'm gasping, begging you for mercy?"

He would. He *really* would.

"Not going to happen," Alberich said, then laughed right in his face. "Sometimes it's brain over brawn, isn't it?" He turned and walked away, leaving Torbin vibrating with anger.

Someday, he would kill him. Torbin didn't know how or when, but it was going to happen.

The bear came to Neve that night, and this time, she

didn't hesitate to sneak out of her room and make her way outside. The emergency exit door was cracked this time, and she wondered if it had been her own desire that opened it, or if one of the staff had been simply lazy.

She didn't really care, though. It had been an exhausting day pretending to not remember anything, and there was something magical . . . mystical about seeing the bear in the moonlight that fed something deep inside her. Neve wanted to be outside, away from the linoleum and scratchy hospital sheets, the scent of disinfectant and the ever-present worry about what she was going to do.

She needed a break.

It waited for her again, patiently sitting outside her window as she approached. Then, to her surprise, it got up and walked toward the forest. She frowned, disappointed, but then it looked back at her as if to ask what was taking her so long.

"You want me to follow you?" she whispered.

Right. She was talking to a wild animal. Perfectly normal.

The bear stared at her until she took a few steps after him, then continued forward. It waited at the edge of the trees until she caught up, then led her into the darkness.

The narrow path wound through the trees; pebbles scattered along the edges of the pine needle-carpeted walkway. Moonlight trickled through the canopy overhead, milky streams winding between the interconnected boughs and splashing weakly on the damp ground. Sweet scents of dirt and rotting leaves, freshly rain-spattered and deep with secrets wafted through the air, mingling with the cool evening breeze. In the distance, the quiet trickle of a stream broke the silence, a musical tinkle harmonizing with the chirp of crickets and the occasional hoot of an owl.

A sharp incline led to a break in the trees, and before Neve lay a small clearing — maybe fifteen feet across — thick with wildflowers now curled in sleep and bordered on all sides by heavy brush. The moon shone more brightly here, casting the area in a soft glow, and the dissipating clouds allowed clusters of stars to appear in the indigo sky like a glittering blanket draped overhead.

"Wow," she murmured as the bear lumbered to the center of the meadow and lay down, watching her.

She walked slowly toward him, then caught a glimpse of something through the brush on the opposite side of the meadow. Curious, she crossed to it and peered through the bracken. A brick wall stood, almost obscured by the vegetation, so tall she couldn't make out the top in the darkness. It extended as far as she could see in both directions.

"I guess Torbin was right," she murmured, then turned back to the bear.

"You realize this is weird, don't you?" she asked it. "You and me? We're different *species.* Not that I'm a bigot or anything, but . . . it's weird."

The bear huffed and scrubbed a paw over its nose.

"Okay, then," she said, walking toward him. "As long as we're clear on that."

It didn't move as she approached, watched as she knelt about a foot away. "It *is* pretty cool, though," she admitted, before reaching out a hand tentatively. "I'm going to touch you now," she murmured. "So, if you'd rather I didn't, just pull away. Don't eat my hand, okay?"

The bear didn't pull away or bite her hand, and Neve smiled when her fingers sank into the thick fur. It was coarse, but softer than she'd anticipated, and when she scratched the bear behind the ears, its tongue lolled out and it almost looked like it was smiling.

"You like that, do you?" she asked, reaching up with the other hand to double-scratch. "Feels good?"

The bear rolled over onto its back, and Neve laughed, surprised. "Really? Belly rubs?"

She rubbed his soft chest, scratching lightly, and the bear let out an appreciative grunt. At least Neve thought it was appreciative. He swiveled his head over to give her a toothy, upside down, bear-grin, so she figured he must have enjoyed it.

It was bizarre, but what in her life wasn't lately? She'd found out she had magical powers, that her doctor was doing weird experiments and *giving* people amnesia somehow . . . what was a belly-rub-loving bear added to the mix?

Somehow, over the course of the next hour, she ended up cuddling with the huge beast, resting her head on his massive shoulder as she looked up at the stars. He was incredibly warm, and actually, a good listener.

"—so I've had to pretend I have amnesia," she told him, summing up the events of the past few days. "And he seems to believe it, but now I'm kind of back to square one, you know? I still have no idea how to convince the others we have to escape, and Torbin . . ." She frowned to herself.

The bear huffed as if to asking her to continue.

"Oh, sorry," she said, reaching over her shoulder to scratch his neck. "I just—I saw him talking to Doctor Alberich today, and it was weird. It was like there was definitely some history there or something. I don't know. I wanted to talk to him, but he practically ran away from me."

The bear was still, and Neve wondered if he had fallen asleep.

"I'm probably being paranoid," she admitted quietly, then decided to change the subject. "Did I tell you I can actually make people *do* things now? Not only conceal myself from them, but make them do stuff. I don't know. It's pretty cool, I guess. Could be useful if I can get a handle on it. And check this out." She held out her hands and concentrated, the sparks coming almost instantaneously now. The bear seemed unimpressed, but Neve didn't take it personally.

"I can do lightning, too. At least, I think I can," she said. "I did once. Kind of." She shrugged and sat up, patting the bear's side. "I have a feeling there's more to it, but I can't quite figure it out yet. I've tried to move things, but not much luck with that. Other than opening doors in the middle of the night, that is. If that's even me." She shot the bear a sideways look. "Is it you?" When there was no response, she shrugged.

"Oh well, I'll keep trying, I guess."

The bear rolled over, and she smiled. "More belly rubs? You're insatiable." She absently scratched at the bear's chest.

"It's probably nothing, right? Torbin and Doctor Alberich?" She smoothed his thick fur, then started to scratch again. "I just worry that the doctor has done something to him. Maybe he's forgotten everything. Maybe he's . . . what's this?"

Her fingers brushed against a rough patch of skin in the center of the bear's chest and she leaned closer, pressing the hair flat so she could see it better in the moonlight. "Is that a brand?" she asked.

The bear didn't move a muscle.

She studied the brand a little closer. It wasn't big—maybe a couple inches long, oval in shape, with a pattern of alternating up and down triangles creating a border around the edge.

"That's odd," she murmured. "Who would brand a bear?" She shot him a look. "And who would you *allow* to brand you?"

He simply stared at her, silent.

She pressed a palm over the brand, then turned to lie back down against him. "I'm sorry that happened to you," she said. "I'm sure it had to hurt."

After a few moments, she yawned, then held up her hand again, studying the sparks along her fingertips. "I know I have to be careful," she told him. "I can't let them know what I'm up to. But I think this is the key. Once I'm strong enough, it won't be about escape. It'll be about taking this place down.

"We need to get out and tell people—the police, the FBI, I don't know. Someone. They need to know what's happening here." She clenched her hand into a fist, extinguishing the sparks. "We need to find proof and take it to the authorities. That's the only way we can really save everyone."

She glanced at the bear. Did he look doubtful? No, that was her imagination playing tricks on her again.

"It'll be okay," she said, yawning again. "We'll figure it out."

Neve wasn't certain exactly when she fell asleep, but when she woke the next morning, the sun was already up, and she was back in her room, tucked into her bed.

Neve had a new purpose, a new goal. If she couldn't convince everyone to escape with her, then she would find a way to get help from the outside world. There had to be a record of what was going on at Blackbriar—medical files, maybe videos from some of those security cameras? If Doctor Alberich was doing experiments, there had to be proof somewhere, and Neve was going to find it.

When she walked into breakfast, she finally felt as if things were looking up.

Tala was back, and although she appeared a bit tired, and ignored Neve and everyone else, she seemed none the worse for wear. Torbin sat across the room, and Neve arched her brows at him, darting a look toward Tala and back to him. The corner of his lips quirked up ever-so-slightly and he nodded subtly, then turned back to his breakfast.

Neve looked away quickly. She didn't need anyone suspecting she was talking to Torbin . . . not when she wasn't even supposed to remember him.

That night, she started a whole new routine. She'd sneak through the halls of Blackbriar, searching for evidence that they could use against Alberich. It was second nature now for Neve to connect to whoever was in the security room, allowing her to slip past the cameras undetected. Any staff members she came across were dealt with in a similar way.

Something told her to steer clear of Doctor Alberich, though. Neve wasn't sure what it was, but with the lack of memories, she was quickly learning to trust her instincts. She'd never set out on one of her snooping expeditions unless she knew where the doctor was. Keeping to the shadows, she'd watch and wait until he'd go down to the basement at night or, on a few rare occasions, actually left the Institute grounds.

The basement, of course, was locked and out of her reach, much to Neve's frustration. But for almost two weeks, she methodically worked her way around the maze of rooms on the main floor.

She thought she'd struck gold when she came across a room full of filing cabinets, but they were all empty. She found a stack of medical charts in a desk drawer, but the pages were all blank. When she was too tired and frustrated to continue, she'd make her way through the forest to the meadow, where the bear would be waiting. She'd curl up next to him and talk, vent . . . sometimes cry, then fall asleep, a hand clutched in his fur, and wake up in her own bed.

She'd never slept better.

Torbin had yet to come near her since she'd been caught by Alberich, and she couldn't figure out why. It was frustrating, seeing him across the room and being unable to talk to him. Unable to ask for his help.

Thirteen days after she woke up with "amnesia"—*again*—Neve sat on one of the benches bordering the lawn, watching him stand and brood in the shadow of the trees. He caught her eye and shook his head slightly, and the frustration of the past weeks swept through her. Neve got to her feet and stalked over to him, hiding them from view of the others.

Torbin stood stiffly, arms crossed over his chest.

"What's going on?" she demanded.

He didn't move.

"You're not going to say anything?" She ignored a flush of embarrassment at the obvious answer to that question. "You ignore me for days and what? You're going to stand there and pretend you don't see me?"

Nothing.

"I need your help. I thought you were going to help me." A rush of anger colored her words, making them sharp and pointed. "Did you change your mind? Did Doctor Alberich change your mind?"

His jaw tightened, but his eyes finally met hers.

To Neve's absolute horror, she choked on a sudden rush of tears. "I need you. You can't turn your back on me." It was pathetic, but she felt so alone. So desperate. Fear and frustration combined until she was almost overcome with despair.

"Please," she begged. "*Help me.*"

A shudder ran through Torbin's body, and he seemed to relax slightly, all his muscles loosening until he finally moved. He reached out with one hand and swept the tear from her cheek, rubbing it between his thumb and forefinger.

Neve blinked up at him, confused. "What's going on?"

He glanced over at the others, then moved past her, pulling her wrist.

"Where are we going?"

He simply waved her forward, miming for her to continue hiding them, and led her through a side door back into the Institute. Neve had never dared to snoop during daylight hours, but she felt safe somehow, having Torbin with her. She realized he hadn't released her wrist, and the touch sent a surge of warmth through her.

Torbin evidently knew exactly where they were going. He led her down the hallway past the common room, to the left, then right, before stopping before a large metal door with a big *No Admittance* sign front and center and a numeric keypad to the right of it.

"Through there?" she asked. When he simply waited, she pushed on the door.

Locked. Of course.

"Can you open it? Like the basement?"

Torbin shook his head, then held out a hand like *go ahead.*

That was Torbin. A man of few words.

"Me?" She laughed. "How am I supposed to open it?"

He pointed to her forehead, then to the door.

"Oh, I don't think —" She chewed on her lip, studying the door for a moment, and remembering that little bolt of lightning running between her fingers. She glanced at Torbin and he simply tipped his head expectantly.

"Okay, here goes nothing," she muttered. She focused, bringing the sparks to her fingers, then tried to focus on the feeling of electricity coming from the keypad. It was different from the lightning — focused and contained, rather than wild and free — but she could feel it now. Actually, now that she was looking for it, she felt electricity all around her. From the fluorescent lights overhead, the outlet near the floor . . . even the security camera at the end of the hall. It trickled all around her, through her, like she was part of a circuit.

Neve held both hands out, palms facing the keypad. She wasn't sure exactly what she was supposed to do, but she focused on the power flowing around her. Maybe she could pull it away somehow—

A surge of electricity burst from the keypad and the door sprang open. She gasped, then paused, eyes darting around everywhere as she waited for an alarm to sound.

Nothing happened.

"Well, that was interesting," she murmured.

Torbin huffed out a laugh.

They went through the door, Torbin pulling it closed behind him, only to come to another door about six feet further. This one had no keypad, no electricity that Neve could detect - simply an ordinary wooden office door with a brass knob.

"What's in there?" she asked Torbin.

He motioned for her to go inside, and she opened the door and flicked on the lights.

It was an ordinary room, wood paneled with brown carpet on the floor. A desk sat before a wall of bookshelves to her right. They were filled with books and a variety of knick-knacks—feathers and shiny stones, candles, and more geodes like they'd found in Tala's room. A rather disturbing painting in dark reds and blacks hung in the center of the opposite wall, a metal filing cabinet standing next to it. It smelled . . . odd. Like a combination of smoke and sweat with a faint tinge of rotten eggs.

"Is this—" She whirled suddenly to face Torbin. "Is this Doctor Alberich's office?"

He nodded but remained just outside the room.

"How did I miss this? This is awesome!" She exclaimed, moving to the desk. "There has to be proof in here, you know? Something we can take to prove to people what's going on here." Neve froze and shook her head. "Sorry, I haven't told you about that, have I? I don't think we can get the others to escape with us, so I figure if we can find evidence of what's happening here, the police will have to listen to us, right?"

She opened a drawer and started to dig through a pile of papers, then glanced up at Torbin. "Are you going to help?"

His body tensed, brow furrowed as if concentrating hard, then he let out a harsh breath and shook his head.

Neve frowned and crossed to him. "What's wrong?"

He shook his head and stepped back, pointing at the door frame in a large rectangle. He stepped forward and held up his hands, stopping short.

"Are you saying—" She tilted her head, thinking. "You can't come in?"

He let out a little growl and tensed again, and

Neve finally realized he was *trying* to come in. And couldn't.

Torbin bared his teeth, the tendons on his neck standing out with the effort. Sweat broke out on his upper lip and every muscle was tight and bulging.

"Stop," she said. "Torbin, stop."

He relaxed, breathing heavily.

"It's okay," she said, then she thought of something. "When you weren't responding to me earlier . . . was it because you couldn't?"

He nodded. *Yes.*

"Because of Doctor Alberich?"

No response.

"You can't answer that?"

He shook his head.

"But how?" As soon as she asked the question, she waved it off. "Never mind. There's no time to get into that now. You stay there and keep watch, okay?"

He nodded, and she went back to the desk. She opened another drawer, but the only thing in it was a book written in some foreign language she couldn't read. The top drawer held pens and pencils—nothing unusual.

"Was it me?" she asked suddenly. When Torbin looked at her in confusion, she smiled. "You couldn't respond to me, but when I asked for you to help me, I wanted it so badly. I didn't mean to manipulate you, but . . . was that what broke the spell, or whatever?"

Torbin froze for a moment, considering, then nodded with a wide smile.

Neve felt a little dazed by Torbin's smile, but she shook it off, crossing to the filing cabinet. "Good to know," she said.

After a few minutes, she slammed the last drawer with a frustrated exhalation. "Nothing," she snapped. "I don't know how a guy who's holding secret medical trials can keep absolutely no records and expect to get grants or funding or whatever, but there's nothing here."

Torbin frowned and smacked a hand against the door frame.

"I know what you mean," she muttered, starting to pace. "There has to be something, somewhere, doesn't there? Maybe we need to get in the basement again or—" She stopped, catching sight of the weird painting hanging on the wall. It was really creepy. Dark and foreboding, but she moved closer to get a better look.

A woman dressed in a filmy white gown lay on a stone platform, her mouth open in a silent scream. A man clothed in black robes stood near her head, a bloody knife held overhead, and Neve realized the woman was a sacrifice. Scores of people surrounded the altar, some laughing, others writhing as if in a corrupt kind of dance. It was unsettling to look at, and the eyes of the man with the knife seemed to follow her as she moved across the room.

*Wait.*

When she looked at the painting from the side, Neve realized there was a gap behind the frame on the left. She pried at it with her fingers and the painting swung open on invisible hinges.

"A safe behind the painting. So cliché," she said, sending Torbin a grin. He looked excited. Hopeful.

Then frantic. He waved at her, pointing back toward the security door.

Someone was coming.

Neve cursed under her breath. They were so close, but there was no way she could break into a safe . . . especially not quick enough to avoid getting caught by whoever was coming. And if it was Doctor Alberich, she couldn't persuade him that they hadn't ever been there. She quickly put the painting back and hurried out of the room, turning off the light and closing the door. Torbin yanked her forward to the thick metal door and hesitated.

There was nowhere else to go. They had to risk it.

He pulled it open just wide enough for them to slip through, then shut it tightly. He started to lead Neve down the hall, away from the approaching voices, but she resisted, holding up a finger.

Neve took a deep breath, reaching for the electricity and placed her palm against the keypad.

It lit up again, restored. Neve wasn't sure if Doctor Alberich would be able to tell it had been tampered with, but maybe it would be enough.

She *hoped* it would be enough.

They took off running, skidding around a corner as she heard the beeps of someone tapping a code into the keypad, followed by the click of the door opening.

*Victory.*

# CHAPTER NINE

They raced around the outer hallway of the building, Neve frantically hiding them from anyone and everything. She bumped a little table, sending a stack of pamphlets flying, and one of the nurses jumped in surprise, looking for the source of the apparent gust of wind that had swept in.

Neve didn't breathe easily until they were back outside. She lifted their concealment long enough for Angelica to notice them both—with a little mental push—then pulled it back over them.

Instead of her usual *Don't see us*, though, Neve tried something a bit more complicated, sending the same thought to all the staff she could see.

*We're both resting in our rooms. No need to look for us. Nothing out of the ordinary.*

It seemed to take, and when Angelica let out a huge yawn, Neve signaled Torbin and they met in their usual spot on the edge of the forest, just beyond the tree line.

"We have to get in that safe," she said, kicking the tree. "There has to be something important in there, right?"

Torbin nodded curtly.

"We were so close!" She kicked the tree again, sending a little piece of bark flying. She eyed Torbin's large, still form. He seemed stoic and unbothered until she looked a little closer. His large hands were clenched into fists, and she could actually hear the spine-chilling crunch as he ground his teeth. He'd led her to the office, and Neve hadn't thought to ask why.

"Do you know what he has in there?" she asked.

Torbin nodded. *Yes.*

"What?"

He gave her a frustrated look and started gesturing in a way that she could make no sense of.

"Okay, okay, hold on." She bit her lower lip in thought. "It's got to be important, right?"

Torbin looked relieved at the simple question. *Yes.*

"If we got it, will it bring him down?"

A slight smile of satisfaction and a slow, deep nod. *Definitely.*

"Can we get to it, do you think? Is it something we can get out of Blackbriar?"

He hesitated, a little unsure.

Neve sighed. "If it's that important, it isn't going to be easy, right? If he went to all that trouble to protect it, he's not going to let us walk out of here with it."

*Yes.*

Neve paced back and forth a few steps, lost in thought as she chewed on her fingernail. "Well, I guess we'll have to deal with it as it comes." She looked up at Torbin, hoping she appeared more confident than she felt.

"First thing is to actually get *in* to the safe," she said. "It's not like that's on my list of skills. You?"

He huffed out a laugh.

"Maybe it's like the keypad on the door? I could suck the electricity out?"

Torbin gave her an encouraging nod.

"That's if it even runs on electricity," she muttered, rubbing the back of her neck. "I didn't get a good look at the lock, but what if it's an old-fashioned tumbler one? Like in the movies? I have nothing to deal with something like that." She took off pacing again. "And you can't get in there to just rip the door off the hinges. Could you do that, anyway?"

He shrugged.

"Maybe I could wish you in?" she suggested. "Like I did earlier. Could my influence overcome whatever's keeping you out?"

Another shrug.

"You're no help," she said, but with a soft voice that let him know she was joking.

She settled on a large log and motioned for him to sit next to her. He perched on it gingerly, dwarfing the fallen tree.

"I'm going to ask you some questions," she said. "Try to get to the bottom of whatever's happening to you. Okay?"

He looked skeptical but nodded.

"What is controlling you?"

He rolled his eyes and she held up her hands.

"Okay, I know. Too broad. Stick to easy yes or no questions." She scrubbed at her face in frustration. "Maybe I can get a pen and paper. Do you think you could write it?"

Torbin shook his head, then clenched his fists, his body going rigid all over.

"That would be a no," she said. "Hard enough to nod, huh?"

He sighed. *Yes.*

"Let's start at the beginning then." She ran a hand through her tangled hair, organizing her thoughts. She could feel Torbin watching her and felt a rush of heat on her neck but tried to ignore it. She had a flash of memory—something bright and happy—and gasped.

"Did you—did you *know* me? Before Blackbriar?"

Torbin let out a relieved breath and nodded. *Yes.*

She pictured the memory in her mind. It was familiar, the one she'd seen before where she was standing with Rose, hands joined, light and sparkles surrounding them. But now, in the background, she saw Torbin's unmistakable large frame, leaning against a tree in his customary pose.

"Do you know Rose?" she asked.

*Yes.*

"So, you don't have amnesia like me."

He shook his head viciously. *No.*

"Then why are you here, no . . . wait." She held up a hand, stopping the open-ended question and re-framing it quickly. "Did you come here at the same time that I did?"

*Yes.*

"And was that years ago?"

*No.*

"So Alberich lied . . . big surprise." She plucked a piece of moss off the log and started to tear it into little pieces. "Alberich took my memories, right?"

Torbin froze, his muscles growing tight, and she tilted her head, studying him closely. "You can't answer that question, can you?"

A jerk of the head. *No.*

"Don't fight it," she told him. "We'll figure it out. Let me think." She paused, sprinkling the moss over her legs.

"That day I woke up, not remembering anything . . . had we been at Blackbriar a week?"

He held out his hands, about a foot apart, then brought them closer together.

"A few days?"

*Yes.*

"So, what does he want with us?" she mumbled to herself. "Do you know what he wants with us?"

Torbin grimaced and held out a hand, palm down, waggling it back and forth. *Some of it. Not everything.*

"Ugh, this is so *frustrating!*" Neve wove her fingers through her hair again, yanking gently. "If only you could—" She froze, focusing on Torbin.

"Can you talk? I mean, normally? Before you came here, could you talk?"

*Yes.*

"So . . . someone took your voice, like they took my memories?" She watched him struggle with the answer, his teeth grinding together.

"You can't answer that," she murmured, pieces starting to fit together. "Anything having to do with Alberich, you can't answer."

Torbin sat stock still, fingers digging into the bark of the tree.

"Alberich," she said distastefully. With a loud crack, Torbin tore out a chunk of the log, crumbling it to a mass of splinters.

"I'll take that as a yes," she said, getting to her feet to pace again. "So, somehow Alberich gets both of us here — he traps us or lures us, I guess it doesn't matter that much, and I'm sure you can't tell me so —" She waved a hand and spun on her heel to walk in the other direction. "He takes my memories to convince me I'm delusional. Takes your voice so you can't tell me what's going on. He's controlling you somehow, even though you're able to fight it to some degree."

She glanced at him, but Torbin was preternaturally still. A confirmation.

"He's got some kind of plan using the patients here at Blackbriar—and I overheard him say that it all leads to me, somehow. It's like he's practicing on the others so he can do *something* to me."

Torbin growled deep in his throat, making her jump.

"Let me try something," she said, sitting sideways next to him, a bit closer now so her knee brushed his thigh. She was painfully aware of the contact but didn't want to make a big deal of it by jerking away.

"I'm going to see if I can break through," she said. "It's kind of creepy, me pushing into your mind. So I don't want to do it unless you're okay with it."

He nodded quickly. *Do it.*

"Okay, I promise I won't do anything weird.

No post-hypnotic suggestions to make you dance whenever you hear the word velociraptor or anything."

Torbin gave her a look that definitely said he was reconsidering giving his permission.

"I said I *won't* do that. I don't even know if I *can* do that. Sheesh!" She did *not* say that it was something she might want to try in the future, when all this was over.

"Okay, try to relax, she said as she rubbed her hands together. "I think—" She cleared her throat. "Maybe if I was touching you? I think it might help."

Without ceremony, Torbin thrust out his huge hands, and Neve placed her palms carefully against his. She closed her eyes and took a deep breath. She'd never tried to influence Torbin before, so she had to find the tether—search for the unique connection—

Wait. It was already there.

Her eyes flew open. "We're already connected."

Torbin's lips curved up in a crooked grin that made her stomach flip.

"Why didn't you tell me?"

He gave her an exasperated look that couldn't have more clearly said, *duh*.

"Okay, okay, cut the amnesiac some slack." She looked into his eyes, the warm brown softening as she stared at him. Neve swallowed thickly, trying to focus on the task at hand. She reached for the tether and put all her will behind her wish.

*Talk to me.*

Torbin's hand tightened on hers and his eyes grew panicked. His whole body tensed up, muscles going rigid, and he bared his teeth, painful grunts escaping in harsh pants. His whole body curled in on itself as if he were in agony, and Neve scrambled to send another command.

*Stop. Stop. Stop.*

He relaxed, breathing heavily.

"Sorry. You okay?"

He nodded.

"Okay, so that didn't work," Neve said. "I could get you to help me, but not to talk. Maybe one command is stronger than another?"

Torbin shrugged, still breathing heavy. *I have no idea.*

"I don't want to put you through *that* again, so let me think for a minute." She still held his hands but pretended not to notice. "I can't overcome the silence command. And I'm pretty sure whatever compulsion you're under to never discuss Alberich is the same."

He simply stared at her, unmoving.

"So maybe we have to be a little creative," she murmured, studying his face for any lingering signs of pain.

There were none.

"Were you ordered to stay away from me?" she asked.

Torbin fought only a moment before he was able to nod. So there was a way to get around the orders. As long as she kept it vague—didn't mention Doctor Alberich by name—Torbin could fight back the compulsion.

"Did that hurt?" she asked. He shrugged like it was no big deal.

Stoic to a fault.

"Can you feel what's been done to you? Inside?"

That question startled him, as if he'd never thought of it.

"It hurts when you push against it, right?" He nodded. "So can you feel it when you're *not* fighting it?"

Torbin tipped his head, brow creased in concentration, and after a moment . . . *Yes.*

"Do the different orders feel different to you? Like, I don't know—can you feel the strength of the unbreakable ones? Others that aren't so strong?"

*Yes.*

"And the order that . . . doesn't let you follow me into Alb—to *certain places.* Is that a strong one?"

Torbin thought for a moment, then nodded

slowly, a grim look on his face.

"Great. I guess I better sharpen my safe-cracking skills."

Neve stared down at their joined hands, and her mind drifted to the earlier memory. She and Torbin had a past of some kind. She couldn't help but wonder what *kind* of past. She assumed they were friends, but could they have been more?

She had a sobering thought. What if the *more* had been with Rose? The idea made her feel a little sick to her stomach.

Torbin released her hand, his finger slowly rising until it touched her under the chin, tipping her head up to meet his gaze. He gave her a questioning look and pointed to her forehead.

She could tell he wasn't referring to her powers this time.

"I'm fine," she said. "Just thinking, you know?" Neve turned sideways abruptly, her legs dangling off the log, and she clutched her now cold hands in her lap. "I, uh, was wondering . . ."

Torbin was silent, but she dared not look at him.

"The memory I have now, of us?" She glanced at him quickly, heat rising in her cheeks. "Of you and me and Rose? Well, I uh, I was wondering. Were you and Rose? I mean, did she—did you—"

Her face was painfully hot now and she yearned to turn back time about thirty seconds, before she dug herself into such an embarrassing hole.

She heard a muffled snort from beside her and snuck a quick look at Torbin to find him fighting laughter.

"Ugh, it's not funny," she grumbled. "It's very frustrating not to remember things, I'll have you know. I'm simply trying to fill in the blanks. But if you don't want to help me—" She got up, prepared to stalk away with what little dignity she had remaining, but Torbin caught her hand and pulled her back.

She slumped back onto the log but didn't look at him. He reached out and gently turned her head, ducking to meet her gaze.

Neve sighed. She supposed it was rude to look away. Like plugging your ears when someone was trying to talk to you.

His eyes were soft, his smile tender . . . unmocking. He very deliberately shook his head back and forth, and relief flowed through her.

"Okay, well, that's—" She swallowed nervously. "That's good to know. You know, for the purpose of making sure my memories are all intact and, uh, accurate—" She swallowed again with an audible gulp.

Torbin simply stared at her, his gaze drifting over her face, as if he were trying to memorize it himself. He still held her chin gently in the curve between his thumb and forefinger. He was so much bigger than her, but she felt no threat. Nothing but an air of protection—of security—emanated from him. Somehow, deep down in her soul, she knew he'd rather die than allow harm to come to her.

"I can trust you," she murmured, the thought forming words without her consent.

He nodded somberly.

"Thank you," she whispered, eyes fluttering closed as she swayed toward him.

A sharp whistle jerked them apart, breaking the spell, and they both jumped to their feet.

"We've been gone too long," Neve said. "We need to get back." She quickly thrust up her concealment, wrapping it around Torbin as they emerged from the forest. They paused for a moment, and she looked into his eyes, a mountain of words silently flowing between them. Hope and fear . . . and promises they both hoped they could keep.

"I'll find you later," Neve whispered, and they took off in opposite directions.

Neve didn't see Torbin again until breakfast the following day. She tried to look inconspicuous, but nerves raced through her as she thought of revisiting Alberich's office that night. Because it had to be that night. There was no more putting it off. Looking around the common room was enough to tell her that they'd probably delayed too long already.

Other than Neve and Torbin, only a handful of patients sat at the tables scattered around the room, dead-eyed as they scooped up spoonfuls of greasy chili. Torbin didn't look in her direction, and Neve followed his lead. Calum stood near the french doors watching them all. She met his gaze and looked away quickly.

Doctor Alberich didn't address the fact that group therapy was down to five patients—Torbin, Tala, Neve, Peter, and Lily. He'd maintained his usual chipper encouragement, scribbling in his ever-present notebook, but Neve doubted he was even listening. When he finally turned to her, asking if she wanted to share, she licked her lips and met his gaze.

"Doctor, where is everyone?" she asked. She could feel Torbin shooting daggers at her but ignored him.

"I beg your pardon?"

"Uh, the group," she said, waving a hand toward the other patients. "Shouldn't there be more people here? Where are Melissa and Nancy? And the young girl with red hair . . . Alice, I think?"

His eyes narrowed on her and she tried to look innocent . . . unthreatening.

He clicked his pen. "I'm not at liberty to discuss other patients with you, but I can say that we've had some successes with our treatment here."

Neve didn't expect that answer and couldn't hide her surprise. "Oh?"

"Yes, we've had a few patients who have progressed enough that they've been able to go home." He closed his notebook and patted it with satisfaction. "It should give all of you hope." He addressed the whole group, but his gaze didn't stray from Neve's.

*Liar.* She hoped her thoughts didn't show on her face. She wanted to press the issue. She *really* wanted to ask about the basement. But Torbin seemed to follow her train of thought and when she slid a glance his way, he gave an imperceptible shake of his head.

Such a small movement, but she knew he was yelling at her in his own, quiet way.

*Don't push your luck.*

She knew he was right. They needed to bide their time and not raise any suspicions. It didn't make it any easier to swallow, however.

"That's great news, Doctor," she said with a smile. "Very encouraging."

He nodded slowly. "Indeed." He stood abruptly. "That's it for now. See you all tomorrow.

Good work." Doctor Alberich turned on his heel and strode out of the room, and Neve let out a long, slow breath. She gave Torbin a weighted look and headed for the yard, strolling toward the forest path as if she hadn't a care in the world. With one quick glance back, she headed into the darkness, feeling it when Torbin followed her. He caught up after a few moments, and she whirled on him.

"Could you believe that guy?" she hissed. "*They've progressed enough that they were ready to go home.* Right. Progressed right down to that creep-show of a basement!"

Torbin gave her a *Tell me about it* look.

"We have got to bring him down. We've got to!" She choked on emotion, and unexpected tears pricked at her eyes. Torbin huffed and pulled her into a hug.

A *hug*. Torbin didn't really seem like a hugging kind of guy.

But he was really, *really* good at it. He was hard all over, but they fit together somehow, and he wrapped her in soothing warmth. His huge hand smoothed over her back, up and down in a hypnotic rhythm, lulling her into a state of peace, or at least as close to peace as she could get in that moment.

Eventually, she pulled back, embarrassed. "Sorry," she said. "I didn't mean to fall apart on y—" Suddenly, her vision darkened at the edges, and the world around her started to spin.

"Oh no," she murmured, and she was aware of Torbin sweeping her up into his arms before the world spiraled away.

The next thing Neve knew, she was in the forest—the dreamy one with spindly trees, unlike the thick pines surrounding the Institute—and Rose was standing before her, a worried look on her face.

"I can't keep this up for long," she said. "He's getting stronger and he's been keeping me out."

"Doctor Alberich?" Neve asked.

"Doctor?" Rose laughed. "That's what he's calling himself now?"

"We're going to get out," Neve told her. "We're going to escape tonight."

"Where are you? I've been scrying, but I can't pinpoint you."

"Scrying?" Neve could see the edges of the vision beginning to swirl. They were running out of time.

"You still don't remember?" Rose reached out and took her hands. "We're witches, Neve. You are a powerful witch."

With that, the memory flashed through Neve's mind of the two of them standing like this, hands joined, as bright light surrounded them. It was clearer now, and Neve could see their heads thrown back, wide smiles on their faces as the light swirled around and through them while sparks danced along their skin.

"I remember," she said quietly. It was true. She was a witch, and she had power. And Rose could help them.

"What kind of power?" Neve asked quickly, the swirling colors were getting closer. "What can I do?"

Rose laughed. "Pretty much anything," she said. "At least when we're together. But the center of your personal power is the elements in nature."

Neve nodded slowly. "Like lightning?"

"Lightning, wind, rain . . . any of it."

Neve looked down at her arm where the snowflake tattoo now shimmered. "Snow?"

Rose grinned. "Snow and ice, yes. You said it's like you're connected to the moisture in the air. The electric current running through everything."

Another tether.

"Can I—" A rush of dizziness swept in and Rose vanished, replaced by Torbin, looming over her prone body. Neve blinked rapidly, and he let out a relieved breath.

"I'm okay," she reassured him. "Let me catch my breath."

After a few minutes, he helped her to her feet and she leaned against a tree, running trembling hands through her hair.

"That really takes it out of you, you know?" she said on a laugh, taking a few deep breaths. Torbin stood next to her, waiting.

"Did you know I'm a witch?" she asked quietly. It was ridiculous. Preposterous.

He nodded. *Yes.*

"Rose, too."

*Yes.*

"She said—" Neve cleared her throat, then got an idea. "Hey, can I show you something?"

Torbin tipped his head curiously.

"Not here, though," she said, eyeing the thick canopy overhead. I need an open area. Come on."

It was much easier to navigate the path during the day, so Neve led him at a quick pace until they reached the break in the trees and the bear's meadow spread out before them. The flowers were open now, a riot of color amidst the varying shades of green. The sun had moved beyond the canopy, but the sky was still light . . . blue and cloudless . . . and an easy breeze ruffled Neve's hair.

"Nice, isn't it?" she asked, walking to the center of the clearing. The grass was matted down here, where she and the bear spent most of their time, and she sat cross-legged on the bent stalks. Torbin approached her, then hesitated for a moment before sinking to his knees.

"Rose says my power comes from nature," she said. "That's why I can connect to electricity."

He nodded. *I know.*

Neve took a deep breath and brought out her sparks, the snowflake tattoo, springing to iridescent life. She felt for the electrical current around her . . . could feel it running through the trees, the ground . . . even Torbin himself. She pulled it into herself, hair standing on end as it permeated her skin, coalescing in a powerful ball, deep in her chest. With a slow exhale, she let it flow to her fingertips . . . and out.

Twin bolts of lightning shot to the sky in a burst of pure, electric power.

Neve gasped. "That—whoa." She turned wide-eyed to Torbin, who didn't look surprised at all.

She frowned. "Have I done that before?"

He smirked.

"You've seen it all, haven't you."

He stretched out on the ground, propped up on his bent elbows, legs crossed at the ankles.

She shifted up onto her knees. "So, can I make it rain?"

Torbin cocked a brow and nodded.

"Snow?"

*Yes.*

"Hurricane winds?"

An eyeroll. *Yes.*

"Well, that could come in handy, I guess." she said. "But I don't think a stiff breeze is going to help us get out of here. Probably should focus on the lightning. Maybe aiming it?"

Torbin shrugged and lay back, his head on his crossed arms.

"Okay, then," she said to herself. "Let's work on that."

They stayed out in the meadow for as long as they dared—less than an hour, Neve didn't think they would go unnoticed for much longer than that—then made their way back the way they'd come. She'd managed to aim the lightning, and control the power of the blast, to a certain extent. It took a lot of concentration, however, so she didn't know if she'd be able to do it while under stress.

And what they planned to do would definitely put her under stress.

"So, I'll meet you later," she told Torbin, stepping over a fallen log. She caught his arm before they left the trees, her stomach churning with nerves. "We can do this, right?"

When he simply arched a brow in response, she sighed.

"Of course we can. We have to."

As usual, they went their separate ways once they emerged in the yard, and it was only when they were on opposite sides of the lawn that Neve let the curtain fall. She entered the common room, surprised to see Lily sitting at a table and reading.

She wasn't looking at her book, though. Instead, she zeroed in on Neve and got to her feet, crossing to her quickly.

"Look," she whispered. "You still kind of freak me out, and I don't know if I can trust you, but you're right. There is something weird going on around here."

Neve's mouth dropped open in surprise.

"I want out," Lily said firmly, a muscle tensing in her jaw. "Can you get me out?"

Neve's gaze darted around the room. They were alone, except for Shelley, the cook, who was tapping away on her phone, not paying them any attention.

"Yes," Neve said quietly.

Lily's eyes narrowed and she lifted her chin slightly. "Then I'm in," she said. "What do you want me to do?"

# CHAPTER TEN

Thursday nights were movie night at the Blackbriar Institute, and although the cinematic selection was generally pretty lame—*Beethoven's 2nd*, anyone?—the lack of alternate entertainment generally meant the common room was packed.

Although packed, in this case, was a relative term. The population of Blackbriar, initially around fifty or sixty patients, if Neve estimated correctly, had dwindled to less than half that. They sat on folding chairs staring up at the shenanigans of Charles Grodin and a rather slobbery Saint Bernard, the staff leaning idly against the wall behind them.

There was nowhere else to be at the moment, apparently.

Neve puffed out a breath, her fingers tapping nervously on her thigh. She glanced at Torbin, who sat off to her right, his elbows on his thighs, fingers tented between his knees as he stared blankly at the

TV. His head tipped ever-so-slightly in her direction, and she knew he was paying close attention to the room, even though he appeared relaxed.

Relaxed for Torbin, anyway.

Neve glanced at the clock.

*Two minutes.*

On their way to the common room, she and Torbin had argued briefly about Lily's involvement in all of this. Neve believed they needed all the help they could get, but Torbin wasn't convinced she could be trusted. Who knew what Doctor Alberich had done to her? How he'd tampered with her mind?

It was a genuine concern, so they'd come to a compromise. Lily's involvement would be limited — and in a way that, even if she wanted to, would be next to impossible for her to double-cross them.

*One minute.*

Lily knew nothing about the details of the plan — only her part in it. At first, she'd balked about being left in the dark, but eventually, she'd accepted it, admitting that if the situation were reversed, she'd probably feel the same way.

*Thirty seconds.*

Neve dared a glance to where Lily sat on the end of the front row farthest from the door. She looked better than she had in a while, actually, the dark circles under her eyes a little less prominent. She sat up straight, alert, her own attention flickering to the clock as she swallowed nervously.

*Ten . . . nine . . .*

Neve's fingers wove together, twisting in her lap, and she reached out to feel for all the tethers in the room — Lily included — gradually building the concealment. Not making herself and Torbin invisible yet, but unnoticeable. Unremarkable.

Boring.

*Three . . . two . . . one.*

Lily sprang to her feet with a wild scream, then picked up her chair and threw it at the television. It cracked and shuddered, then broke free of the wall, dangling by the power cord. Neve watched in awe as she grabbed another chair and threw it across the room, narrowly missing hitting a patient in the face. She danced away when Calum tried to catch her, ducking under his arm and stepping from one empty chair to another, then onto a long table along the back wall, holding the evening's snacks. She picked up a bowl of popcorn and threw it toward the kitchen, and Neve jumped when someone grabbed her arm.

Torbin was giving her his patented *Are you kidding me?* look.

*Right. The diversion.*

With one last look over her shoulder at Lily, who had jumped over the back of one of the orderlies and was tossing out Oreos to cheering patients, Neve strengthened the camouflage over them and they ran out of the room. They ducked into a small alcove and waited, the shouts from the common room getting even louder. If Lily did her job — and so far, it appeared she was doing it *very* well — the other patients would be joining the melee now. Neve took a moment to send a general *wreak havoc* message along the tethers and the noise level increased.

But it still wasn't enough. Not until they were certain the coast was clear.

Torbin stood next to her, so close she could feel the heat off his arm, the in-and-out of his breathing. The seconds seemed to tick off in slow motion, her heart pounding faster with every one.

*Where was he?*

It seemed like minutes, but in truth, it was probably thirty seconds at most before Doctor Alberich passed them at a run, heading toward the common room. Neve smiled. So far, so good.

With one last push for the residents to keep up the mayhem, she and Torbin ran in the opposite direction, toward the doctor's office. Alberich should be kept busy for a while breaking up the fights, then making sure the patients all got to their rooms.

Neve hoped it would be enough.

Thunder rolled outside and Neve looked up in

reflex. "Storm's coming," she murmured, feeling the electricity gather, even inside the building. It tickled along her skin, but also somewhere deep inside her chest, as if there was a storm building there as well.

Neve didn't waste time with the keypad, using the electricity to fry it completely. There was no need to try and hide their tracks. This time, it was all or nothing. She strode to the office door, but instead of opening easily, it was locked.

"Crap," she muttered. "Can you deal with this?"

Torbin approached the door and reached out, wrapping his beefy hand around the knob. His whole body tensed, teeth grinding, biceps bulging with effort. He grimaced in pain.

"No, stop," she said, reaching out to touch his arm.

Torbin pulled his hand away and shook it out.

"You can't go in, right?" she asked, purposely not mentioning Alberich's name.

Torbin shook his head. *No.*

Neve chewed on her lip, studying the door. "But if you yanked the doorknob back, you wouldn't be going in, right?"

He looked confused, but she smiled.

"Do you think you can break it off?"

At that, Torbin's mouth curled in a slow grin. He strode forward and grabbed the knob again. He braced himself, then gave it a twist and a good, hard yank.

It ripped a hole clean through the thin office door, which drifted open with a creak.

"Nice," she told a still-grinning Torbin. "Okay, my turn."

The lights were on, various books and papers strewn across the desk, as if the doctor had been working when he was summoned to the common room. Neve shuffled through the items, trying to make sense of what she was reading.

"Some of this is in another language," she told Torbin. "Latin and something else I don't recognize." There were some diagrams, notes about weather patterns, phases of the moon . . . what appeared to be a list of ingredients: Blackthorn, Adder's Tongue, Crushed Bone, Magnetite, Blood . . .

*Blood.* Neve swallowed nervously.

"I don't know what this guy is cooking, but it's seriously creepy," she murmured. Torbin made an impatient sound, and when she glanced at him, he waved toward the safe.

"Okay, okay," she said quietly, turning around so she could pull the painting out on its hinges. She studied the safe for a moment. It wasn't large, maybe one-foot square, brushed steel with a black handle on the left.

Nothing else. That was it. A flat surface with a

handle. No lock. No keypad. Nothing.

"Perfect," she muttered. She hadn't gotten a good look at it before, but she'd assumed there would be *some* way to open it.

"There's no lock," she told Torbin. "I don't know what to do!"

What had she been thinking? She was no detective . . . no superhero. And now she'd put all of them in danger, for what? Poor Lily. Neve couldn't even imagine what she —

Torbin smacked his hand hard against the wall, jolting Neve out of her frantic thoughts. He pointed to the safe, then to Neve, then very deliberately covered his eyes.

Neve's eyes narrowed. "You think — you think he shielded it somehow, like I do? Disguised it?"

Torbin shrugged. *Maybe?*

"Well, that tricky little . . ." She placed a hand on the safe door and closed her eyes. Sure enough, she could feel the familiar buzz of electricity beneath its surface. Neve inhaled deeply, collecting the power around her and the lights flickered. She intended to send a burst through the door, as she had with the keypad earlier, but she noticed something she hadn't before. She could actually *feel* the circuits . . . how they worked, the way the electricity was controlled and diverted by them.

So instead of frying everything, she let out a mere trickle of power. The door buzzed and shimmered, and suddenly, there was an electronic keypad next to the handle, followed by a telltale click. Neve grabbed the handle, and the safe door opened easily.

"I can't believe that worked." She shot a stunned look Torbin's way before reaching in to pull out a small bag made of soft, black cloth. It rattled slightly, and she opened it, pouring the contents onto the desk.

It was an odd collection of items—some obviously valuable, others mere trinkets to Neve's untrained eye—a small wooden cross, a medallion carved with the head of a wolf, a silver coin, a blue teardrop earring, an old key. There were a few gemstones as well, the largest appeared to be an emerald, oval in shape and about two inches long. She held it up between her thumb and forefinger.

"This is probably worth a pretty penny," she said, but she couldn't keep the disappointment out of her voice. "I don't know how any of this is going to help us, though."

A strange sound caught her attention, and when she looked at Torbin, she couldn't believe the anguish in his eyes as he stared at the emerald.

"Torbin? What is it?"

He pointed at the gem, then at his own chest.

"This?" She held it up. "It's yours?"

Torbin nodded, pulling the necklace he wore

from under his shirt. She'd seen it before—when she first came to Blackbriar—but only now realized that the center of the pendant was recessed.

As if something was missing. A stone.

An *emerald.*

And given the insanity of her life lately, Neve had the strongest feeling that it wasn't a simple emerald. There had to be more to it. Could the emerald be the key to breaking whatever control Alberich had over Torbin?

He held out a hand, eagerly waving her forward with the other.

"Okay, hang on," she said, sweeping the rest of the items back into the bag, in her haste knocking the key onto the floor. It bounced under the desk, and she tucked the emerald into her pocket, dropping to a knee to retrieve the key, slip it into the bag, and pull the drawstring closed. She was about to put it back in the safe, but Torbin made another sound, indicating she should bring the bag with them.

"Really?"

He pointed at the bag, then back the way they'd come. And it all clicked into place.

"Are you saying Alberich stole all of this?" she asked. "From the patients?"

Torbin didn't respond. Couldn't respond. So she knew she was right.

"What a—" She pressed her lips together and

shook her head. "Never mind." Neve quickly closed the safe and swung the painting back into place, figuring the longer it took Alberich to realize he'd been robbed the better. She grabbed a few of the papers off the desk—the ingredients list, along with a few of the more disturbing drawings and diagrams.

"I hope this will be enough," she said, rolling them up and sliding them into the bag. She hurried toward Torbin and had her fingers wrapped around the emerald in her pocket, about to pull it out and place it in his outstretched hand—

—when his eyes rolled back into his head and he slumped to the ground in a heap.

"Torbin?" She fell to her knees, dropping the bag on the floor as she touched his face. "Torbin? What's wrong?"

Then she saw it—Two coiling wires led from Torbin's shoulder, curling across the floor and up . . . to a taser held by Doctor Alberich. He stood, flanked by Calum and Angelica, with his hand wrapped tightly around Lily's knobby wrist. She didn't even fight against him, her eyes wide and vacant, and a sick feeling roiled in Neve's stomach.

"What did you do to her?" she demanded.

Instead of responding, Doctor Alberich strolled toward her, a smug smile on his face. "I'll take that," he said, pointing to the bag with the taser before he dropped it on the floor. "And don't try any of your little tricks or your friend here will have a most unfortunate accident."

"Don't hurt her!" She slid the bag across the floor, and he stopped it with his foot.

His eyes widened. "I wouldn't hurt a patient," he said mockingly. "She might, however, hurt herself, if it's suggested." He addressed Lily now. "Pick up the bag."

She bent down woodenly and followed his orders.

"Stand on one foot." She did.

His black eyes took on an evil gleam. "Kill your friend."

Lily's face twisted and she bared her teeth, lunging toward Neve. "Just kidding!" the doctor said with a laugh. "Don't kill her. I have need of her."

Lily relaxed back into her slumped posture, eyes glassy and unseeing.

"Interesting, isn't it?" He shot a look at Neve. "She'll do anything I say. Anything. So if you want to keep your friend in good health, you'll get up and come with us. There's a good girl." He watched with satisfaction as Neve got to her feet, then jerked his head toward Torbin, who was coming to, groaning on the floor.

"Get him up."

Calum and Angelica grabbed him by his arms,

heaving Torbin to his feet. He stood, shaking his head to clear it, then glared at Alberich.

"Ah, yes. There's my little lapdog," he said.

Torbin saw the bag in Lily's hand and his eyes fluttered closed, shoulders falling in defeat.

The emerald. He didn't know that Neve had it.

"Torbin," she said, waiting until he met her gaze. "It's going to be all right." She flicked her eyes down and made a fist in her pocket around the stone. Torbin caught the movement and nodded slowly, then looked away.

"Isn't that sweet," Alberich said, rolling his eyes. "But I'm afraid there's no time for a lover's reunion. Off we go." He gestured for her to proceed out to the hallway, followed by Torbin—Calum and Angelica close on his heels—and finally the doctor and Lily.

"So what now?" Neve asked through gritted teeth. "You drug me again? Give me *amnesia*?"

Alberich laughed. "Oh that time has come and gone, I'm afraid." They headed down the hall, then around the corner, and Neve knew they were going to the basement.

"I have to hand it to you," the doctor said. "You had me convinced you'd lost your memories again. How did you do it?"

Neve lifted her chin stubbornly.

"No matter," he said, grabbing her elbow with his free hand as they turned another corner. Torbin growled, but Alberich shot him a quelling look. "Really? Haven't we moved past the theatrics yet, Torbin? Move."

She saw Torbin fight the command, then he exchanged a significant look with Neve before continuing on the way. She could see the anger and hatred burning in his eyes.

"I'm okay," she said quietly.

"Of course you are," Doctor Alberich said, pulling her down the hallway, past the rest of the little group. "I wouldn't hurt you. I need you. You're kind of the point of all this, you know?"

"What—" She stumbled as the basement stairway came into view, and a chill of fear ran down her spine. "What are you going to do to me?" The gemstone bounced against her thigh with every step as they made their way down the stairs.

*Let us go. Let us go. Let us go.* Neve figured it was worth a shot.

He gave her an arch look. "Haven't you figured out yet that you can't bewitch me?" He huffed. "It's pathetic really. I expected more."

She glanced back and caught Torbin's eye over her shoulder. He looked murderous, fists clenched by his sides, but he made no move to act on it. Calum and Angelica exchanged a look behind him and she wondered if they were fully aware of the doctor's plans or simply going along with them.

What had he promised them? Or maybe they

were being compelled as well?

Alberich entered a number in the keypad and shoved open the basement door, dragging Neve alongside him. "I would have liked to have both of you, you know," he said in a conversational tone. "But your sister is rather slippery. Better to take you one at a time, anyway. Wouldn't want to lose both simply because I've been a little greedy." He shot her a wicked grin, and she gasped when she saw the sharp points at the edges of his teeth. She blinked and they were smooth and even once again.

Alberich laughed but didn't share the joke.

Neve reached for her sparks, willing a jolt of lightning through her arm into his hand, but his grip only tightened. "Stop that," he hissed. "It tickles."

They passed room after room of hospital beds, and Neve realized many of the missing patients were there, either unconscious or sedated.

"Are they all right?" she asked, spotting Nancy, the crochet lady, in one of the beds.

"So concerned about them," he replied. "You should be more concerned about yourself. It's your greatest weakness, you know. That's how I got you in the first place. Using your big friend here as bait."

Neve glanced at Torbin, whose gaze fell to the floor, his shoulders slumping in shame.

"If you hurt them . . ." She gave Alberich a hateful look.

The doctor jerked her to a stop, his grip on her wrist bruising. "What?" he snapped. "You'll what, exactly? Can't you see that you are not in control here, little girl? Not anymore."

They glared at each other for a long moment and Neve longed to creep into his head and make him jump out a window or something. He smirked, as if he could read her mind, then turned and stalked away, pulling her and Lily along with him.

They entered a room similar to the one they'd found Tala in, but much larger. A hospital bed sat in the center surrounded by candles, and Alberich shoved her toward it. "Use the restraints," he told Calum. "This could get messy." He left Lily hovering near the door next to Torbin, whose entire body pulsed with his desire to do something—*anything*—to get them out of there. The pendant hung empty against his chest, like a frame without a portrait.

There was something about it . . . something she couldn't quite put her finger on.

A dozen other people lined the room—staff, she would have called them an hour ago, dressed in scrubs, a few wearing stethoscopes. Neve was now certain they weren't personnel, however. They seemed eager, wild light burning in their eyes, and she was reminded of the creepy painting hanging in Alberich's office.

Neve had the sneaking suspicion that she was

the sacrifice.

Her mind raced as she searched for a way out. Could she get the others to attack Alberich? Or were they under commands like Torbin and Lily, and any effort to influence them would prove fruitless?

Calum pushed her roughly onto the bed and reached for the wrist restraints. Alberich's back was turned, so she risked connecting to Calum's tether.

*Loose* she thought. *Make them loose.*

Calum faltered for only a moment before buckling the restraints, and Neve had to make an effort not to smile when he followed her instructions. It wouldn't be evident to anyone watching, but she could easily slip free of the bonds should the opportunity arise.

She was even able to convince him to skip the leg restraints altogether, tossing a blanket over her ankles to hide that fact.

"All right," Alberich said, raising his hands. "Let's begin." He clapped once and the candles burst into flame as the overhead lights blinked out. The observers edged closer, their eager faces twisted and eerie in the candlelight. Thunder clapped and Neve could feel the storm outside. She remembered the weather charts on Alberich's desk and wondered if that was why he'd chosen this moment for whatever was going to happen.

Neve reached out, searching for a connection to

one of the observers. Perhaps she could be quick and stealthy enough to get one of them to knock Alberich out before he noticed.

But she couldn't find a tether.

She reached out to Calum, usually so easy to detect, but he eluded her as well. It was as if the circle of candles blocked her ability, limiting her power to its boundary.

Now Doctor Alberich was the only one within reach, and he was immune to her. He swiped a damp finger across her forehead, then over her heart, leaving a reddish streak on her T-shirt.

*Blood.* It had been on the list in his office. Neve shuddered.

A low rumble echoed through the room, and Neve realized the observers were chanting. She couldn't make out the words, it was something in another language, guttural and rhythmic and it grew louder and louder until it echoed in her heartbeat. Alberich hovered over her, black eyes gleaming as he joined the chant, holding the geode in one hand, and an empty bottle in the other.

A rush of panic surged through her.

*Now.* She had to run now. Neve went to slip out of the restraints but found that she couldn't move. She was paralyzed, frozen in place as Alberich's voice took on a deeper timbre that vibrated through her, piercing her chest.

Her chest was glowing.

"What's — what's happening?"

Alberich's gaze took on a manic quality as he continued to chant, moving the bottle closer to her. The light emanated from her chest in a solid beam, winding up and away, then curving down and into the bottle.

"Do you feel it?" he asked in that deep, terrifying voice. "Your power ebbing away? It will be mine soon. All of it. First yours, then your sister's."

She could feel it. Something tearing deep inside her. She writhed, arching up, as if her body couldn't bear to let it go.

Neve screamed, agony and instinct reaching out, clawing at the electricity around her — the storm outside — gathering it up, and turning it loose.

Lightning flashed, bursting through the room in a crackling tangle and the candles blew out, the chanting coming to an abrupt stop as everyone around her fell to the floor. Neve inhaled sharply and the power draining into the bottle reversed quickly, plunging back into her.

Neve was overwhelmed, a little dazed, but she couldn't risk hesitating. She slipped her hands from the restraints as Alberich got to his feet.

"Stop her!" he shouted, and Calum stumbled forward.

Instead of heading for the door, Neve ran full

speed toward Torbin. It took a moment for Calum to react . . . just long enough for her to crash into Torbin and slip the emerald from her pocket into his.

"Oh, for heaven's sake." The doctor glared at Calum as he yanked Neve back toward the bed. "If you can't handle the job, I can give it to someone else." He fumbled with the book she'd seen in his office, running a finger down the page. "Now we'll have to start over."

"I've got it," Calum muttered, dragging her along. Neve made a big show of crying and moaning like she was in pain.

Causing a distraction.

"Please don't! It hurts so much!" she shouted as Torbin realized what was in his pocket.

"Would you shut her up! I'm trying to concentrate!" Doctor Alberich didn't look away from his book. The observers got to their feet with groans and hateful looks in Neve's direction.

"I'll do anything you want!" she begged, as Torbin turned his back slightly to hide where he pressed the green stone into his pendant. Nobody noticed the shimmering glow that emanated from it, encompassing Torbin from head to toe before it vanished.

"Please!" She slumped onto the bed. "Don't tie me down again. I can't stand it!"

The doctor finally turned and approached her.

"Good heavens, what a whiner," he said distastefully. "When did you become so pitiful? What happened to the—" He continued to drone on, but Neve wasn't listening.

Instead, she fought to keep from screaming out loud as Torbin took a huge stride into the circle, then in the blink of an eye his body twisted and morphed, hair sprouting all over him as he grew two feet taller. His mouth extended, melding into a snout, the pendant resolving into a glowing, green mark on the center of his chest.

His furry chest.

Torbin was gone, and in his place stood the bear. The bear Neve had spent her nights with in the meadow, a brand burned into his skin, now shimmering with green light. The bear that she now knew had watched over her, just like Torbin.

Because it *was* Torbin.

With a furious roar, it raised a paw, and Doctor Alberich didn't even have a chance to turn all the way around before Torbin backhanded—*backpawed*?—him across the room.

Everyone froze in surprise, and Torbin used the confusion to change back and grab Neve's hand. "We need to get out of here," he said.

"You—you can talk?"

He grinned at her but didn't bother answering as he caught her up in his arms and ran out of the room, scooping up the bag of talismans on the way.

# CHAPTER ELEVEN

They only got a twenty second head start. Thirty, if you pushed it. Neve could hear Doctor Alberich shouting, the others in the room rushing out in pursuit, and clung to Torbin's neck as he took a corner at breakneck speed. The door leading upstairs was just ahead, and he yanked it open with one hand before setting her on her feet at the base of the stairs.

"Go!" he shouted as he slammed the door closed.

Neve raced up the stairs and spotted a push broom propped against the wall.

"Torbin!" She tossed it to him and he wedged it through the door handle and took the steps two at a time.

"That won't hold them for long," he said, taking her hand as they raced toward the main entrance. Hopefully, there would only be one or two people watching the front desk and she'd be able to get them out. She still felt a little woozy, though, after whatever Alberich had done to her, so she hoped she was up to the task.

Okay, a *lot* woozy. She stumbled and fell to her knees, the room spinning around her. Torbin swore, and quickly swept her up in his arms, then ducked into a small storage room. He set her down and pushed her hair back from her face, studying her with worried eyes.

"I'm okay. Sorry," she muttered, blinking to try and fight off the dizziness. "I don't know what's wrong with me."

"Someone just tried to steal your power, that's what happened," he said with gritted teeth. "Are you in pain?"

"No," she replied. "Just lightheaded. We don't have time for this. We need to get out of here." Neve started to get up, but Torbin stilled her with a gentle hand on her shoulder.

"Give it a minute," he said quietly. "You can't do anything if you pass out."

She nodded, breathing in and out slowly, and reached out to touch his pendant.

"That's how he did it?" she asked. "The emerald?"

Torbin nodded, still looking worried. "It enabled him to command me, to a certain extent," he replied. "He couldn't keep me from shifting—not at night, anyway—and he couldn't completely keep me from you. Our ties are too strong."

Neve's cheeks heated at the implication. "And the others?"

"He used the talismans to control them, muddle their minds. Each item is precious to its owner . . . a focal point of their own particular magic. It must have taken years for him to collect them all."

It took a few moments—way too much time in their present situation, but gradually, Neve's mind cleared and she got to her feet.

"Can you walk?" Torbin asked, his arms twitching as if he was prepared to carry her again, if necessary.

"Yeah. I'm okay. Let's go."

Torbin tilted his head for a moment, listening, then opened the door, leading her toward the front entrance at a quiet jog.

They skidded around the corner and Neve gasped in surprise. A group of patients stood before the door, blocking the way. Nancy was there . . . Peter and Melissa . . . the young girl Alice. All had glassy eyes and vacant expressions and were armed with an odd assortment of weapons—broken bottles and metal pipes, pieces of wood and little Alice held a shovel, of all things.

"What are they doing?" Neve asked as the

group walked slowly toward them.

"Can you control them?" Torbin asked.

Neve tried, but the effort sent a sharp pain through her head. "I can't," she told him. "Whatever Alberich did, it's still affecting me."

Torbin's jaw tightened, and Neve knew he was weighing going through them by force.

"We can't hurt them," she said, touching his arm. "It's not their fault."

Torbin nodded shortly, then tipped his head at the sound of approaching footsteps. "Come on," he said, pulling her down a side hallway. They ran through a meeting room and out the other door, down another hall and through a pair of swinging doors. Torbin pushed one open and held up a hand.

Neve froze and he tilted his head, listening.

"Can you hear anything?" she whispered.

"I'm not sure."

They walked through the doors and Neve realized they were across from the common room. If they could get out into the yard, maybe they could find a way around the building. Torbin had apparently reached the same conclusion because he took her hand and nodded toward the common room door.

"Ready?" he asked.

She nodded and they hurried quietly across the hall, listening carefully for any sounds of pursuit.

They pushed through the door and shut it

quickly behind them, not daring to turn on the lights.

"We really have to stop meeting like this," Doctor Alberich said wryly, a flash of lightning lit up the room, revealing the doctor and all the others who had been in the basement. He sat in the center of the group, legs crossed as if he hadn't a care in the world, but his cheek and right eye were swollen from Torbin's blow. Neve took no little pleasure at that. Lily huddled in a corner, chewing on her thumb. Neve reached out for her, but her tether was so weak . . . barely a thread.

Rain pounded on the ceiling and another bolt of lightning cracked, sizzling through Neve's nerve endings. She fell back a step, uncertain where to run.

Alberich laughed at Neve's shocked look. "All of this," he waved a hand, getting to his feet as Angelica flipped on the lights. "All of this and you forget about the cameras? Really, Neve, that was sloppy of you." He shook his head and snatched the bag out of her hand.

He was right. She'd completely forgotten about the cameras. Hadn't even bothered trying to hide.

What an idiot.

Thunder rumbled and Neve felt another flash of lightning burst through her. It left a tingle behind, racing up and down her body, and she felt stronger, somehow, as if it were re-energizing her.

Torbin stretched up next to her and morphed into the bear, falling to all fours in front of her to shield her from Alberich. He bared his teeth and let out a spine-chilling roar. Alberich hesitated, then pointed to his left where Calum stood, holding a rifle.

"It may not kill you. Not at first," Alberich said. "But I'm pretty sure it'll cause some damage." When the bear growled, Alberich nodded and Calum swiveled to aim at Neve.

"Think hard, beast," Alberich said, with a grimace of distaste. "Can you kill me before he kills her?"

After a moment, Torbin shifted back. He took Neve's hand, still angled slightly before her, blocking her from Calum's rifle.

Neve's heart sank. They had nowhere to go. Maybe she could call the lightning again, but how many innocents would be hurt?

"There's no fighting this, Neve," Alberich said, mock pity in his voice. "I've been working on this for so long, taking power from so many, but it's all been in anticipation of you."

"That's what you've been doing to everyone?" Her gaze drifted to Lily . . . to Tala and Nancy . . . before she turned back to Alberich. "Experimenting on innocent people so you can steal my power?"

Calum moved sideways to get a better shot. Torbin growled.

"You still don't understand, do you?" Alberich said, shaking his head. "I needed to capture enough magical power to complete the ritual. They—" He waved his hand toward the other patients—"were good enough to oblige."

Neve couldn't follow. "Magical?"

"They all have power," Torbin said through gritted teeth.

"What?" Neve blinked at him. "You mean like—like you? Or me?" Neve asked.

"Some of both. Some other," he replied. "This *creature* brought them all here, has been doing so for several years. We knew, but didn't understand why. You and I were tracking him when we were taken."

"You did get close, didn't you?" Alberich said with a self-satisfied grin. "But as they say, *no cigar.*"

Thunder shook the windows.

"Now that I've perfected the ritual, I can take it all." He turned to face his followers . . . his slaves . . . "We will take it all."

"Is that what he told you?" Torbin asked them. "That he's going to share the power with you? He won't, you know. You can't believe anything he says." He shot Neve a weighted glance and she sent out a subtle push.

*Don't trust him.*

"Of course I will," Alberich said, waving a hand dismissively. "These are my brothers and sisters. We share everything."

Still, a rumbling murmur ran through the others. Torbin seemed to sense it, too. He eased toward the french doors slightly.

Neve pushed a little harder. *He's lying to you.*

"Why would he share it with you?" Torbin asked them, taking another small step, keeping himself between Neve and Calum. "You know him, right? When has he ever sacrificed anything?"

The murmurs grew louder.

"What is he saying?" one of the men asked, and Alberich whirled on him.

Torbin and Neve took a step, then another.

"He's saying nonsense, of course," the doctor replied.

Then, without another word, he snapped his fingers at Calum, who pivoted and shot the man in the chest. He clutched his shirt, eyes wide, and dropped to the floor.

"Anyone else have questions?" Alberich asked, surveying the room in a long, slow circle.

Neve and Torbin stood frozen, still a good four feet away from the french doors. Alberich's followers slid to the side, cutting them off, and Neve saw the other patients who'd been guarding the front door move into the room through the opposite door.

They were surrounded.

Torbin squeezed her hand and cut his eyes toward Alberich.

"You really are a pain in the neck," Alberich said, but Neve wasn't sure if he intended it for her or for Torbin.

"Ready?" Torbin asked under his breath.

"For what?" she hissed back, but he was already gone. He dove at Alberich's legs, knocking him down, and the bag skidded across the floor. He rolled, pulling Alberich over him, a shield as Calum tried to find a shot. Then, with a mighty heave, Torbin shoved Alberich toward Calum and scampered across the floor.

"What are you doing?" the doctor shouted. "Shoot him!"

A shot rang out, ricocheting off the wall. Torbin grabbed the bag and tossed it to Neve. She fumbled, clutching it to her chest, then ran toward the kitchen in Torbin's wake. He threw people aside as they came toward them, then reached back for Neve, sliding her through the pass through.

"Do it!" he shouted, blocking the entrance. He fought like a wild beast—which Neve supposed he was—but she had no idea what she was supposed to *do.* "Use them!"

"I don't under—" Then it clicked.

The bag. She crouched under the pass through

and pulled open the drawstring, peering inside.

*He used the talismans to control them . . .*

The emerald had broken Alberich's hold over Torbin. Could it be that a cross and an earring and handful of rocks could help her break his control over the other patients? She felt the truth of it as the thought crossed her mind. These items gave Alberich his control. They were the tether to his victims.

And now Neve could use it.

She gripped the bag and closed her eyes, reaching out not for a single tether, but for all of them, a web of tangled strands leading to each one of the others. She could feel them now, their confusion and anger . . . imprisoned in their own minds.

Neve took a deep breath and wished with all her might, sending out a single command through the web, two simple words that encapsulated everything she wanted . . . *needed* . . . them to do.

*Be free!*

Everything was silent for one, long moment. Then the shouting started up again, and when Neve peeked over the counter, it took a moment for her to realize what was happening.

The patients were fighting back.

Not only were they fighting back, they'd discarded their makeshift weapons. Whatever control Alberich had was gone, and the power he'd been so envious of now had free rein.

Tala bared her teeth and her body shifted, transforming into a large, black wolf. She lunged at Calum, who dropped the rifle and scampered for the french doors. Nancy threw up a hand, and Angelica flew across the room, slamming into the wall. Little Alice floated in the air, chasing one of the orderlies out of the door. All of Alberich's allies followed suit, the doctor himself leading the retreat. The kitchen door flew open and Torbin rushed in.

"Are you all right?" he asked.

She nodded. "Yeah, I'm fine."

"Then let's go finish this." He took her hand and they raced outside.

Fighting raged on the rain-soaked lawn as lightning flashed overhead. The wind roared, whipping Neve's hair about her face, and she could feel everything—the electricity surging through the air, humidity weighing on her skin. Torbin released her hand, transforming into the bear in the blink of an eye, and he roared, jumping into the melee. He threw bodies aside and they crumpled to the ground, shouts and screams mixing with the roaring thunder and howling wind.

Neve saw Calum pick up a discarded pipe and move toward the wolf form of Tala. She shouted a warning that was swallowed by the storm. Lifting her hands, she called on the lightning and it crackled down at the man in a flash.

His hand fell to the ground still clutching the pipe. Calum stared at the cauterized stump, frozen in place, and Tala whirled, fangs bared. She leaped onto the man and Neve lost sight of them as the crowd closed in around them.

It was a battle of strength, both physical and magical. Neve paused a moment to watch in awe as a panther lunged at a man who vanished, only to appear right behind the animal and grab it by the tail. Alberich's followers did have some power of their own, but what they didn't have was months of pent up frustration and rage, finally set free.

Neve spotted the doctor himself on the far side of the lawn, running around the side of the building.

"Torbin!" she shouted, taking off after him. "Alberich's getting away!"

The bear shoved his way through the fight, leaving in his wake a tangle of limbs and broken bodies littering the ground. Neve flung a bolt of lightning toward Alberich, narrowly missing him as he disappeared into the shadows. She called on the storm, feeling it pulse through her body as rain dripped from her hair and sparks danced around her fingers, and she could feel the heat of the snow tattoo throbbing under the wet sleeve of her sweatshirt.

She slowed to a stop, searching the darkness for signs of the doctor, and Torbin pressed into her side. She tangled her fingers in his fur, gaining strength from his warm presence.

"Do you see him?" she whispered.

Torbin tilted his enormous head, listening, then took off at a run.

"I'll take that as a yes." Lightning lit the sky as she chased after him, and Neve spotted Alberich running toward the front of Blackbriar. He whirled, throwing out a hand, and Torbin was knocked off his feet. Neve reacted on instinct, sending a bolt of lightning toward the doctor and he whipped his hands up to block it. Some kind of shield protected him from the lightning's full impact, but the impact did push him back. He dropped to the ground and rolled, springing up quickly to dash around the corner.

Torbin roared, the enraged sound sending a chill down Neve's spine, and melded back to his human form.

"I don't know if I'll ever get used to that," she said through heavy breaths as they chased after the doctor. "How did he do that anyway? I thought all the power he stole was given back."

They splashed through puddles on the cracked asphalt, then a loud crack sounded overhead. Torbin wrapped his arm around Neve's midsection and dove away, curving his body protectively around her as a pile of bricks fell to the ground where they'd been standing.

"Good question," Torbin replied. "Creatures

like Alberich have a certain amount of power, but not enough for a shield like that."

"*Creatures* like Alberich?" Neve asked. "What kind of creatures?"

They got to their feet and edged toward the pile of bricks slowly. Torbin shot her a look.

"They're called many things," he said, edging forward to peer around the corner. "Brownmen. Bogles. Duergar. I just call them monsters."

Neve gulped.

"His control was terminated." Torbin continued as he scanned the area. "Whatever you did restored their memories. Reminded them of who they are. I guess that was enough for them to regain their abilities, but perhaps Alberich was able to retain some residual power."

"Like a magical battery," Neve murmured.

Torbin shrugged. "Batteries run out," he said, before leading her around the corner. They moved quickly but quietly now, unsure of what waited for them. Torbin held up a hand, tipping his head, and then Neve heard it, too.

Voices.

"—be reasonable." That was definitely Alberich, and he wasn't alone. Neve and Torbin exchanged a look and jogged to the end of the building and around the corner.

The front gates of Blackbriar rose ten feet tall, twisted iron with arrowhead points bridging the gap in the brick wall Neve had first seen in the meadow. Alberich stood backed against it, his hands held up defensively, as the patients of the Institute surrounded him.

They didn't look happy. They also couldn't get to him. Whatever shield he held stood firm against their attack, repelling fists, weapons, even fire shot from the hands of . . . *was that mousey Peter from group?*

Neve and Torbin made their way through the crowd, coming to a stop a few feet from where Alberich huddled against the gates. He perked up when he spotted Neve.

"There you are," he said. "You have to stop this!"

Neve cocked a brow and crossed her arms. "And why would I do that?"

"Because—because I can help you!" He nodded rapidly. "I know how to return your memories. You want them, right? I'll give them back."

She shrugged. "I don't really want them that badly."

The crowd laughed, and Peter shot a fireball at the shield again. It bounced off, but Alberich seemed to shrink a little.

As a matter of fact, did he look shorter? A little hunched at the shoulders?

"You can't let them kill me, Neve. You're not a

murderer!"

Neve approached the shield, eyeing the spot where she imagined it to be. "I might be. I can't really remember."

Then, she heard the strangest sound, and the crowd fell quiet. A soft melody traveled on the gusting winds. Neve didn't understand how she could even hear it over the storm, but there it was. The tinkling notes seemed to float through her body, relaxing every muscle, and a gentle feeling of contentment descended over her. Over all of them.

Well, except Alberich. He whimpered behind his shield, although Neve really couldn't be bothered with him at the moment.

The crowd parted, and Neve saw for the first time where the music was coming from. Lily walked slowly toward her, the otherworldly song flowing from her lips.

"Lily," Neve said, her own tongue feeling thick in her mouth. "Are you all right?"

The song stopped, its echo still hovering over them, and Lily smiled, touching Neve's cheek. "I'm fine," she said. "Thank you for helping me."

Neve nodded and watched, dazed, as Lily approached Alberich. She reached out and pressed a hand to the shield, tilting her head as she considered him.

"You're right, you know," she told him. "Neve's not a murderer."

Alberich swallowed, his eyes wide with fear. His hands trembled and Neve could tell that Torbin was right.

Batteries run out.

Lily's lips twisted in a wicked grin. "She's not," she said. "But I am."

"Cover your ears," Torbin hissed.

Neve barely had time to comply before Lily opened her mouth and let loose a bloodcurdling scream. It vibrated in Neve's bones, sending her to her knees, and pierced through Alberich's shield, knocking him into the gates. Lily drew closer to him, the scream echoing off the walls, the trees . . . cutting through the thunder and lightning itself, and Alberich fell to his knees, his own hands pressed to his ears. Neve could see blood dripping from under his fingertips.

"Stop!" he cried, but nobody could hear it. His face twisted in agony and he crumpled to the ground, writhing for a few long, painful moments before he finally grew still.

Lily closed her mouth with a smile of satisfaction.

The silence seemed to echo around them for a moment, then the quiet patter of raindrops filled the emptiness.

Shakily, Neve got to her feet and Torbin wrapped an arm around her waist to steady her.

"Are you all right?" he asked.

She nodded. "What happened? What did she do?"

"Lily's a siren," he replied quietly. "We're lucky she can control that scream, or we'd all be dead."

"That was control?" Neve rubbed her ringing ear, then slowly approached the pink-haired girl who'd been her first friend at Blackbriar.

"Lily?"

The girl glanced up at Neve, then they both looked down at Alberich. As blood pooled around him, Neve watched his body shrink and bend.

"What's happening?" she asked.

Alberich's hands grew gnarled and twisted, his chin jutting out to an outrageous point and his aquiline nose expanding, a sharp bend making it almost hawklike. His black eyes seemed to shrink under his protruding brow, and as the life flowed out of them, Neve saw his true form for the first time—bent and crooked. Dark and twisted.

"Nasty, isn't he?" Lily said with a sniff. She turned to Neve and held out a hand. "May I have my earring please?"

It took Neve a moment to realize what she was asking, to remember she still clutched the black bag in her fist. With trembling fingers, she held it out to Lily, who reached in and retrieved the teardrop earring. She hooked it in her left ear, and with one last smile, turned and walked away without another word. The crowd parted again silently, then closed behind her with voices and fists raised in victory.

Behind Alberich's still form, Blackbriar's gates swung open.

Neve stood frozen for a moment, then she realized nobody was moving.

"The talismans," Torbin said, his voice low and encouraging. "You need to give the rest of them back."

"Oh! Of course." Neve fumbled with the bag, pulling it open quickly. She took out the silver coin and held it up. "Whose is this?"

Tala stepped forward, the black wolf now the beautiful woman. Her head held high, she held out her hand, letting out a little breath of relief when Neve dropped the coin into her palm.

"Thank you," she said, and Neve could see the emotion behind the words in Tala's eyes.

"You're welcome."

Tala glanced at Torbin. "I see you got your voice."

He smiled. "I see you got your wolf."

She tilted her head with a small smile and walked past them through the gates.

Neve cleared her throat, feeling heat rise in her cheeks. "Were you two—"

Torbin rolled his eyes. "We're *friends*," he said. "You never used to be this jealous."

Neve bristled, but then he gave her a teasing

wink, and she couldn't find it in herself to stay irritated. Instead, she turned to the line of Blackbriar's former patients and handed out the rest of the talismans.

Then, Torbin took her hand and squeezed it gently and they followed them out. As soon as they passed the gates, he straightened, looking around with a surprised look on his face.

"I know where we are," he said. "I can't believe we've been so close to home all this time."

Neve opened her mouth to respond, but a sudden rush of electricity surged through her and the next instant, Rose appeared before her.

"We've found you!" she said. "I don't know what happened, but one second you weren't anywhere, and the next, there you were!"

Neve realized it was another vision, and Rose hadn't magically transported to her. She smiled at her sister. "We got out," she said. "Everyone is free and Alberich's dead."

Rose let out a relieved sigh. "Thank heaven," she said. "Don't worry, we're on the way. I should be there soon."

Neve looked to Torbin, who was watching her with something soft and gentle in his eyes, and she smiled.

"It's okay, stay where you are," she told Rose. "We're coming home."

# EPILOGUE

She recognized the house as soon as she saw it. Sitting on the edge of a small farm, it was the home of her memories, a little house with a broad front porch . . . a barn to the left with a fenced area for the chickens. A garden, bright with life and color.

Torbin was right. All this time, they hadn't been far. It had taken only a few hours to find the way. They hadn't slept a wink, but neither seemed to mind.

"I don't know why I'm nervous," Neve told Torbin as they stood at the end of the gravel drive. "It's not like I've never met her before."

Torbin, still the strong, silent type, even though he had his voice back, simply squeezed her hand. "It'll be all right."

She nodded and they started down the drive as Rose emerged from the house, a wide smile on her face.

"I think she saw us coming," Torbin said, and . . . of course.

*Of course* she had.

Rose squealed and raced down the drive, dark hair flying behind her, glinting red in the sunlight. Neve glanced at Torbin, chewing her lip.

He released her hand. "It's okay," he said. "Go ahead."

Neve nodded and took a few more steps before Rose swept her into a tight hug. "You're here!" she exclaimed, taking Neve's face between her palms. "Are you all right?"

"Yes." Neve took a moment to examine her sister's face in person. It was less ethereal than in the visions, more solid and real. She had the same sprinkle of freckles over her nose as Neve, the same slight lift at the corners of her eyes. Again, she marveled at how they looked so similar, but also so different.

"You still don't remember," Rose said, frowning slightly.

Neve shrugged. "The others got their memories back. I thought maybe when Alberich died, but . . ." She shrugged again.

Neve had returned all the talismans, but there was nothing for her in that little black bag. No gem. No trinket. Torbin had said there was nothing like that for Neve, that Alberich had to resort to drugs blended with magic to erase her memories.

And unfortunately, he knew of no remedy.

Neve forced a smile for her sister. "I guess I'll have to make new memories."

Rose reached up and touched her cheek gently, giving Neve a glimpse of the rose tattoo. "We'll see about that," she said, then she reached out and took Neve's hands.

"Open your mind to me," her sister said with an encouraging smile. "You know how, right?"

Neve nodded and closed her eyes. She reached out and found Rose's tether right away, like it had been waiting for her all along.

"That's right," Rose murmured. "Just like that."

Neve felt the tingle of electricity running through her and opened her eyes to find sparks dancing along their joined hands . . . up their arms. A bright light glowed between them, growing bigger . . . and bigger . . . enveloping them both in a dazzling display of light and color.

She squeezed her eyes shut, then the memories hit.

Neve saw Rose running beside her, as a child, then a teen . . . working with her in the garden, washing clothes, playing tag. The memories whirled around her, layering on each other with no rhyme or reason—they were toddlers, sitting at their mother's knee, then women holding a large spoon, together stirring a potion to aid headaches. They ran through the forest, waded in the creek, and always . . . there at the edge of her vision, was Torbin.

Keeping watch. Protecting them both.

She saw him bringing her a bouquet of

wildflowers, eyes lowered as he smiled shyly. Reaching out to touch her cheek as they stood in the moonlight. Felt his strong arms around her, the touch of his lips as he kissed her for the first time.

The first of many times.

And above it all, she felt the love — the love of her sister like a subtle breeze, blowing over all the memories of their lives together.

The love of Torbin — *for* Torbin — crashed over her like a wave in a raging sea.

Neve's eyes flew open as the light around them dimmed, until all that remained were a few twinkling sparks around their hands before those too, slowly winked out.

"Are you all right?" Rose asked, dark eyes concerned.

Neve inhaled and let out a trembly breath. "I remember." She reached out and wrapped her arms around her sister's neck, holding her tight. "I remember," she sobbed, and Rose rubbed her back in long, soothing strokes. She cried tears of relief, of regret . . . letting go of the horrors of the past few months and rejoicing that she'd found her way home.

"He wanted us both," Neve said, finally understanding exactly what that meant. "If he'd gotten us both--"

Yes, Neve had power. She now realized how much, and it was considerable. But when she and

Rose joined together, they became more than the sum of their parts. Together, they created some of the strongest magic in the world.

*That* was what Alberich had ultimately wanted. And he'd come so close.

"It doesn't matter now," Rose assured her with another tight squeeze. "It's all over. He's gone."

Neve pulled back, swiping at the tears. "I'm okay," she said, then looked around. "Where's Torbin?"

Rose touched her cheek again—a now-familiar gesture. "I imagine he wanted to give us some time."

Neve smiled and hugged her sister again. "I'm glad," she said. "But I—"

"—need to see him," Rose said with her. They were always finishing each other's sentences. Neve remembered that now.

She laughed. "I'll be back."

"You better," Rose said. "I made a pineapple upside down cake for lunch."

"My favorite!" Neve said with glee. She remembered her favorite dessert!

"I *know*." Rose rolled her eyes and headed back toward the house.

Neve knew where Torbin would be. She headed down the path behind the barn that wound through the trees, the sun streaming through the canopy and dancing along the undergrowth. Torbin never liked to be too far away from them, but sometimes he needed his solitude.

His cave — Neve teased him endlessly about hibernating, regardless of how many times Torbin insisted he didn't need to — was partially shielded from view by a curtain of vines.

Neve approached slowly and called out, "Torbin?"

She heard a rustle of movement from behind the curtain, and a moment later, the bear emerged. Torbin found his bear form relaxing. Human thought was pushed aside, and he operated on instinct and hunger. The world was smaller, as a bear. Sometimes he needed that.

But right now, Neve needed to talk to the human Torbin. "Could you change back?" she asked.

A moment later, he stood before her, tall and brave and beautiful. "Everything okay?" he asked quietly.

Neve cleared her throat. "I remember," she said.

Torbin took a step toward her, then stopped. "That's — that's good. Rose helped you then?"

Neve nodded. "Torbin." She rushed toward him and jumped into his arms. "Thank you."

He rubbed her back. "There's no need —"

She pulled back and he set her on her feet.

"You were there," she said, reaching up to touch his scruffy cheek. "You were always there watching out for us. For me."

He clenched his jaw. "When I couldn't do anything. When he stopped me—"

"It doesn't matter. He's gone," she said, and suddenly, she had to make him understand. "Torbin, I know now what we meant to each other . . . what we *mean* to each other," she said. "But I want you to know, I didn't need my memories to know that I love you."

He stilled, meeting her gaze.

"I loved you before I *knew* I loved you." She let out a little laugh. "That sounds crazy, but—"

Neve was going to say more, to tell him how important he was to her, how grateful she was to have him . . . how she never wanted to let him go.

But Torbin didn't give her the chance. He pulled her to her toes and took her in a deep, bruising kiss, and every thought flew right out of her head. She reached up to tangle her fingers in his thick hair, breathing in his scent as their bodies pressed together—hard to soft—and she let out a soft gasp when he broke away, chasing his lips with her own.

"I love you too, you know," he said, breath warm against her skin. "I always have." He cupped her face tenderly, his gaze showing her everything now. "Always."

Neve smiled up at his handsome face, looking down at her with such adoration it made her heart ache. She thought of all the times they'd had together, and all that lay ahead, a warm satisfied feeling settling in her limbs.

"I know," she said, and the truth of it drew them together again.

After a while—a long while—Neve took his hand and led him out of the forest. "Rose has pineapple upside down cake," she told him.

Torbin groaned. "I've missed that."

Neve laughed, joy overflowing. "Me too."

They emerged into the sunlight and walked hand in hand toward home. Whatever lay ahead, Neve knew they'd always face it like this.

Hand in hand. Side by side.

"What are you thinking?" Torbin asked, lifting their joined hands to press a kiss to the back of hers.

Neve shrugged. "Nothing much. Only that I love you."

Torbin grinned and pulled her close. "There's no *only* about it," he said. "That's everything."

And with that, he pulled her into another deep, drugging kiss.

Neve was pretty sure they were going to be late for lunch.

She was also *definitely* sure that she didn't mind at all.

# ALSO BY T.M. FRANKLIN

**The MORE Trilogy**

*"Reminiscent of the Mortal Instruments series . . .*
*only better!" - Penny Dreadful Reviews*

MORE
The Guardians
TWELVE
MORE Trilogy Boxset

**The New Super Humans**

Super Humans
Super Powers
Super Natural
Super Heroes
Super Humans Boxset

**SWEET ROMANCE, WRITTEN AS TAMI FRANKLIN**

**Love in Holiday Junction**

Falling for Her Best Friend

Of Snow and Roses

Falling for Her Biggest Headache
Falling for Her Opposing Counsel
Falling for the Wrong Guy

**Six Sweet Short Stories, all with a HEA**
. . . And Then They Fell in Love

**Standalone Stories**
Cecilia's Soulful Heart
How to Get Ainsley Bishop to Fall in Love With
You
Cutlass

**Magical Holiday Romance**
Second Chances
Visions of Sugar Plums

# Acknowlwdgments

This book was inspired by a favorite fairy tale of mine from childhood, *Snow White and Rose Red*, so a huge thanks to the Brothers Grimm, whose work lives on more than a century later . . . and to Marjorie Cooper, who illustrated the version I read over and over when I was a little girl.

Thanks so much to Melissa Storm and the awesome team at Sweet Promise Press for inspiring me to write this story.

Thanks to my wonderful editor, Kathie Spitz, and my awesome proofreader, Rose David at Rose David Editing.

Thanks to Lindsey Gray for the beautiful formatting.

Special thanks to the awesome readers at The T.M. Franklin Book Club. You guys are amazing!

And of course, thanks to my wonderful family for their never ending support.

# ABOUT THE AUTHOR

T.M. Franklin writes stories of adventure, romance, & a little magic. A former TV news producer, she decided making stuff up was more fun than reporting the facts. Her first published novel, MORE, was born during National Novel Writing month, a challenge to write a novel in thirty days.

MORE was well-received, being selected as a finalist in the 2013 Kindle Book Review Best Indie Book Awards, as well as winning the Suspense/Thriller division of the Blogger Book Fair Reader's Choice Awards. She's since written novels in a variety of genres, as well as several best-selling short stories...and there's always more on the way.

T.M. also writes sweet romance as Tami Franklin.

Printed in Great Britain
by Amazon